The Superpower

Philip Machanick

Copyright © Philip Machanick 2020

Master Jack lyrics courtesy Hidden Years Music Archive, Stellenbosch, South Africa

Cover art copyright © Philip Machanick 2020, based on a collage of free photos on Unsplash by

- ruddy.media https://unsplash.com/@ruddymedia
- Pedro Lastra https://unsplash.com/@peterlaster
- Vlad Gorshkov https://unsplash.com/@nuclearvee

Author:	Machanick, Philip, 1957-
Title:	The Superpower / Philip Machanick.
Publisher:	RAMpage Research, 2020.
ISDN.	978-0-620-90347-9 (pbk.)
Subjects:	FICTION / Science Fiction / Action & Adventure

Other titles by this author:

- *MIPS2C: programming from the machine up*, 2015, ISBN 978-0-8681048-7-4
- *The Day it Rained Forever*, 2013, ISBN 978-1-4825609-9-2
- *No Tomorrow* (2nd edition), 2008, ISBN 978-0-9804510-1-6
- *An Object-Oriented Library For Shared-Memory Parallel Simulations*, 2008, ISBN 978-0-980451-02-3

Contents

CONTENTS

It's a strange, strange world we live in, Master Jack
You taught me all I know and I'll never look back

Chapter 1

Kurt's office

Someone is hammering on the door. Kurt turns from his work on the chalkboard behind his door to face an unexpected visitor, annoyance lightly suppressed.

"Jack. What do you want?"

"You upset my wife."

"Did I? Jane told me a while back that she broke her nose in an accident. I asked her yesterday to remind me how. She forgot. You don't forget how you broke your nose. So I asked if you did it. Did you do it?"

"You interfering asshole. How dare you?"

Kurt gets up and walks up to Jack, now just inside the doorway.

Eyeball to eyeball, an arm length away, Kurt says, "I dare because she is my friend and you are a bully."

Jack swings a punch at Kurt. Kurt steps inside it, knee to groin, bunched fingers to solar plexus, crunching headbutt to forehead in short order. Jack doubles up.

Kurt follows up. "Hitting girls is pretty low but any sign of any bullying, you answer to me. And next time, I might just let that punch land and give me a case for real self defense. Now fuck off out of my sight."

Jack turns tail and vanishes.

Kurt calls after him, "I thank you, Master Jack."

Jack's disappearance reveals a student – Jamie. Kurt's expression softens.

"Next! What can I do for you? Jamie, isn't it? Big classes are kinda impersonal..."

"Uh, I was thinking of asking for an extension on my assignment but maybe..."

"Relax. That treatment is strictly for bullies. The assignment is a warm up. You must be looking at it the wrong way if you need more time. Show me what you have so far."

"I'm good in the lab but this computer stuff... I don't know where to start. I guess you get that a lot from biologists trying to do your course."

Kurt grins. "Bioinformatics is the new kid on the block. Some day all biologists will learn coding along with wet lab techniques. I was lucky. I started with computer science before I did biotech. I still sometimes forget that you wet lab types find coding tough." He leads Jamie to his office chalkboard and hands him a piece of chalk.

"Go on, write up your starting point."

"What was that Master Jack thing?"

"Oh, just words from an old song. The guy's name happens to be Jack. Means nothing. But sort of weird that it's the president's name as well. He for sure would relate to being called 'Master'. In a bad slave-owner way."

Kurt focuses. "You're not here for that. Show me where you got stuck."

Jamie writes.

Then there's another knock on the door, much less frenetic than Jack's. Kurt turns. The door obscures Jamie from the new visitor. "Colonel, we need you."

"Allen Kingston! It's been a long time. I go by professor now, General. Why do you need me?"

"Haven't you been watching the news?"

"It may have escaped your notice but I have a day job."

Kurt walks to his desktop computer and opens a web browser to a news channel: Breaking World News, BWN.

He turns up the sound in time to catch an anchor announcing, "Latest is the president is not harmed. We review what happened this morning."

The view switches to the Rose Garden, where President Jack is at a podium, talking with his usual agitation.

"Thank you, but that is FAKE NEWS. I am not taking a follow up. You had your question. You! I don't know you, who are you?" The president points at a mangy-looking person in the middle of the media crowd.

"Harper. Thomas Harper, Canadian News Network."

"Canada? I hope you are nice, not like our fake news crowd."

"Absolutely, I hope so too. Apologies for my nerves – it's my first time at the White House. Should I move closer?"

"Yes, yes. Let him move closer so I can hear him properly. I think he's NICE."

Harper pushes through the press corps right up to the podium. Without warning, an orange-brown fluid sprays into the president's face. Secret service are all over Harper and the president disappears.

Kurt closes the web browser. "OK, but it all looks under control. Why do you need me?"

"Because it is *not* all under control. Did you get the name of the person who sprayed the fluid?"

Kurt says, "No, should I know him?"

Kingston says, "Local security contractor, in the Canadian alien camp, disappeared for a while. Reappeared after a month or so. Claimed he lost his memory."

"Oh, right. Didn't he try to fly one of their dropships and crashed it?"

"That's right. We put a lot of resources into figuring out how he did that because humans usually can't use alien tech. Keyed to their DNA, we guess."

"And?"

"There was a rumour that he had turned into one of them after an accidental contact with their tech. He denied it and it seemed implausible. But now the president is changing into one of them."

"So I'm..."

"... the only person with clearance to know this and with top-rank biotech smarts."

"And that clearance level is...?"

Kingston looks puzzled. "Top. Strictly need to know. Obviously."

"Obviously. But... You just read in one of my students."

Kingston finally sees Jamie behind the door doing impressions of a goldfish out of water. Chalk very slowly drops out of his hand and the crack as it hits the floor is like a rifle shot in the stunned silence.

"Damn." Kingston looks grim." Kid! You will have to go with us."

"My assignment..."

Kurt shakes his head. "Jamie. That's the least of our troubles right now. Don't worry, you will just have to lay low until this goes public and that can't be very long.

"Meanwhile you'll have to tag along for the ride. And it will be quite an experience."

It's a very strange world and I thank you, Master Jack

Chapter 2

Kingston's car

The usual Washington DC traffic build up hasn't started yet so they make smooth progress. The general drives his SUV, official black but nothing to distinguish it.

Kurt breaks the silence. "OK general. Explain now. Why me?"

"Two purple hearts, two PhDs. Who better?"

"Cut the crap. There has to be more to it than that."

"Harper's story needs to be checked out. Urgently. If true, we have a major crisis on our hands." Kingston looks at Jamie.

Kurt frowns. "Yeah, right. Need to know. But I *need* to know. ASAP. If this is really serious I need max time to think. Jamie knows the gist now and could be some help."

Kingston nods slowly, taking in the need to bend the rules. "OK. OK. Harper claims the stuff he sprayed on the president is a *cure*. Reverses the alien contaminant that turned him into one of them. And, he claims, there is some sort of contaminant that will make one of them look human,"

"So the president. . . "

". . . is one of them. If this checks out. Which I do not believe for an instant but we need independent verification. You see the problem?" Kingston focuses on the traffic while Kurt sinks back into his seat, deep in thought.

As they hit a higher-traffic zone, police outriders appear with flashers and sirens on. Their motorcade cuts through the traffic.

Jamie stares at their escort. "Wow. This suddenly got real."

Chapter 3

White House

President Jack is sitting at his desk looking even more annoyed than usual. But perfectly fine. Until he thumps the desk with a hand that is looking slightly insectoid at the fingertips. Kingston walks in, followed by Kurt and Jamie.

"Mr President. General Kingston. You may remember me from..."

Jack rounds on him. "Look at my damn hand! This is treason! Except they tell me a foreigner can't be charged with treason! Pathetic!"

"Mr President, Professor Kurt Lowell is the best we've got. Top scientist. Four tours in Afghanistan. Top security clearance, no delay to read him in."

Kurt adds, "Mr President, I have never hesitated to serve before. This is going to be a tough one, particularly as it's strictly need to know. Easier to bring my equipment here than to do this in the lab."

Jack indicates Jamie. "And who's that?"

Kurt introduces Jamie. "Student. I need one person to help with the lab work and there's no time to find someone cleared at this level. I can vouch for him."

Jack stares at Jamie. "You better be right. I will be back from Saudi and Israel by the end of the week. Now get out, I need to prep for that trip."

Kurt and Kingston are striding fast through more corridors of the White House than Jamie knew existed. But he is struggling to keep up and has no time to pay attention.

Jamie says, "How can you...?"

Kurt grins. "... be sure of you? I didn't survive four tours of Afghanistan and get all that fruit salad on my uniform by making poor judgements under pressure. General, can we see that Canadian accused of attacking the president?"

Kingston nods, barely breaking stride. "Sure. I can take you straight to him. Meanwhile do you have a shopping list?"

Kurt says, "For sure. Jamie, can you make notes as we go? We will need the portable DNA sequencers from my lab for a start... and you had damn well better be good in the lab."

Jamie gets a sense of panicked scenes, people walking fast without obvious purpose. He isn't sure what they will be doing but, whatever it is, Kurt doesn't seem to lack purpose.

Chapter 4

Interrogation room

Thomas Harper is on one side of a table with a lawyer, Cy Campbell. Kurt is on the other side with FBI agent Clive Mannon. There is something a bit off about Campbell – a turquoise tinge to his skin and hair but that could be an artefact of the light.

After introductions, Kurt says, "OK, things are moving fast. I need background. Are you planning on cooperating?"

Harper nods. "Of course. There is no time to waste. Your president is an alien."

Mannon looks doubtful. "Why are we supposed to believe that?"

Harper responds, "Did you never wonder why his skin is a weird colour and his hair looks like plastic? And he keeps forgetting things he should know. Which he covers up by lying about everything."

There's a long pause. Kurt fixes him with a gaze. "Actually that is less surprising than you would think."

Campbell chimes in. "My client is not an American so he may be unaware of how easy it is to fake an identity in this country. No national identity scheme, and how often is a politician asked to produce their birth certificate?"

"Actually Canada is not so different, and I grew up in this country," Harper protests.

Campbell ignores this. "Instead of investigating my client, who has been happy to wait on your convenience, why don't you investigate your president's past?"

Kurt turns to Campbell. "Good points, but the president's past is not my department. I am just here to provide scientific back up to check out Harper's claims. Agent Mannon?"

"I can't comment on where else the investigation is going. I am, however, intrigued as to how your embassy provided a lawyer so fast."

"We monitor breaking news. It was obvious he was a Canadian with potential for an international incident. I am on standby for just this sort of eventuality."

"Canadians regularly attack US presidents?"

"OK, Jamie, let's not get distracted. I'm the science on the team and you're here to back me. I do biochem, biotech, DNA and so on. I have a lab that can do fast DNA sequencing and I can code faster than most, so that is what I am here for. And my gear is mostly portable, so I can set up wherever I need to work." Kurt turns to Harper. "Quick summary. No waffle, give me intel I can work with."

"I'm searching for alien tech and find a lab in the camp. Something leaks onto me. Antonio... alien, we give them human names, their language is too hard, says he can cure me but I must get to the mothership. I try and get shot down. I slowly turn into one of them. My hands go first. Then slowly the whole body. Another time, with no one watching, I manage to get onto the mothership and meet Antonio. He gives me the cure. More than I need so I bring some home with me. Then they land me back home – making sure no one sees. Tell me they want no drama. Suits me."

There's a long pause. Harper looks shaken.

Kurt says, "Good, keep going. It does check out. No other human has ever been able to make alien tech work, not so?"

Mannon nods and Harper goes on. "Then Antonio disappears and his son Juan comes to me. There is a faction. They saw how their tech turned me into one of them. Worked out how to do the reverse, make one of them look human. Same basic tech, just somehow works in reverse. And got him elected as your president. So easy, just spend I think... hundred thousand dollars, Facebook ads. Totally confused the competition."

Kurt rolls his eyes.

Harper holds his head in his hands.

Kurt prompts him. "Go on, we need you to talk."

"Juan worries that Antonio is dead. No one knows for sure. That alien was a real friend, looked out for me, kept his word."

"I get it. Serving in Afghanistan has a way of making you appreciate true friends. And some of them were Afghans. Problem is, I need something to work on. All we have is your word and the fact that you squirted something on the president and he is apparently morphing into an alien. Well, his hands are changing, which is a start on that trend."

Mannon squeezes in a question. "How fast does this thing progress?"

"For me, the hand went fast. The rest of the body maybe a week, two weeks. Changing back, about the same."

Kurt adds, "Whether it will be the same for the president, we can't say. But it is an indication. We do not have a lot of time."

"A lot of time for what? If he turns into an alien..." Mannon looks grim.

"... and claims the aliens did it to him? I am not sure what we do with it but knowledge can only help."

Harper wrinkles his brow. "You say you do DNA and so on. I know nothing about that. But can't you check the president out? There must be something..."

"Are you holding my client? If so, I need to know the charges so..."

Kurt says, "Sorry, not my department, Mr Campbell. I'm a science advisor, not law enforcement. For his own safety I would prefer to keep him here. And so I can also question him again. Agent?"

"We can hold him as long as you like and almost certainly longer. Until we have evidence to the contrary, this is an assault on the president and that is serious even if there is no permanent damage."

"Well, I need him to be kept safe. I also need a DNA swab."

"Of course. Go ahead." Campbell does not look happy at this concession but doesn't intervene.

"And a sample of the fluid he sprayed on the president. Agent, do you have that?"

Mannon nods. "We have that. Would a DNA sample from the president be helpful if we can get one?"

"Of course. But if the story is true, will he cooperate? And if not, how will he take it if we treat him like a suspect?"

"Good point, which is why we preserved his water glass as evidence. I hope the sample will be big enough." Mannon passes Kurt a glass in an evidence bag.

"It may be – but also contaminated from others handling it."

Chapter 5

Makeshift lab

Kurt and Jamie are in a small cluttered room. It contains the usual lab stuff such as test tubes and reagent bottles as well as a few small electronic devices. DNA sequencers aren't what they used to be; these babies fit in a pocket.

Kurt is reading a display. "We need more reads to be sure but the Harper guy's DNA looks close to standard, just some oddities. Probably residue of whatever the alien contaminant did to him. But nothing that should affect function. President's DNA is seriously weird. Best we check to be sure. I am going to risk asking him directly for a swab."

Jamie is working on one of the sequencers and pauses to ask, "Should I run the fluid again?"

"Naah. Lots of random organics but something there that's clearly an RNA virus with some very weird proteins. But not like anything we know. If this is the mechanism, it would take a lot of lab time to work out how it attacks DNA."

"And we don't have the time?"

"Maybe we do. But I need to know that first. If we do, good. If not, I will officially give up and carry on working at home."

"Why are you telling me this?"

"Because you, kid, are read in on it and I need help from someone. I just hope you are up to it."

Chapter 6

Israeli briefing room

The scene shifts to Israel. Two US flags are in the background along with numerous Israeli flags. Two central chairs are empty, with Israeli functionaries seated around the empty seats. Jack and the Israeli Prime Minister Mishlakhes stride in. Cameras click furiously.

Jack announces: "I just got back from the Middle East." Israeli advisor eyeroll. "But you all know I've just been in Saudi Arabia." Jack and the Israeli PM sit.

Jack says, "I also had a good discussion with Prime Minister Mishlakhes. On board with what Saudis want. Great for America, lots of money."

Mishlakhes says, "Yes, fantastic, we see eye-to-eye." He turns to Jack, who needs no encouragement to plough on into a minefield.

"Israel has a right to a final solution for the Palestinians. Final solution!" Jack gestures expansively as he says this.

Chaos erupts in the press corps.

"Mr President, Judith Kushner, *Israeli Post*. Any idea what you just *SAID*?"

"Sure, Israel has a right to a final solution..."

"... and that is what Nazis said about Jews. Final solution. Should we be using that kind of language? Are we on that side?"

Jack seems to miss the point. "You know me! I see good in people on all sides!"

Chaos turns to pandemonium.

Mishlakhes tries to bring things back to order. "I think we are missing the point here. This is not World War II. America is our friend."

Another reporter is heard over the affray: "So Nazis are a good side now?"

Mishlakhes sees there is no good way out of this but out. "Mr President, I know you have to catch your plane. I can stay for a few more questions."

Jack takes his leave amidst shouted questions.

The Israeli Post Reporter calls out: "Prime minister, does it not bother you that he speaks in such obvious anti-Semitic tropes?"

Mishlakhes purses his lips for half a minute. "It is not anti-Semitic if a friend of Israel says it."

Chapter 7

Alien camp, Canada

A dry, dusty plain – part of the Canadian Prairies – sits near the US border. The mothership is overhead. A high perimeter wall is topped with an electrified fence. Razor wire surrounds a gate with a heavy presence of armed guards and a machine gun nest. A convoy passes through. US-Canada Security armoured personnel carriers, painted black with USCS logos emblazoned, file in. The APCs are given close air support by a helicopter in similar livery.

The convoy passes rows of untidy shacks with filth everywhere. Aliens scatter, showing no sign of motivation. The convoy stops in a cloud of dust at a shack. There is nothing special about it.

USCS contractors pile out of the lead vehicle and form up, weapons ready. Captain Rivera takes the lead. He bashes on the door. The door opens.

"We know there is alien tech here. Against the law! Hand

it over and there will be no trouble."

The alien is clearly agitated and points past Rivera, to his right.

A giant walking war machine is heading their way and kicks the hindmost APC into the air as if it is a football.

Rivera yells, "What the fuck!"

USCS contractors flee in panic, while the sky is lit up by blue beams from the shack, answered by the war machine. There are mighty explosions and more APCs fly through the air. The chopper beats a hasty retreat. APCs that are still drivable follow, then USCS contractors who only have the option of decamping on foot, doing a passable imitation of an Olympic sprint.

Chapter 8

Oval and out

Kurt, Kingston and top military brass file into the presidential presence.

Jack is pacing in front of the Resolute Desk. "When the hell are you going to fix this? I can only stay out of sight a few days. I have rallies... If I wear gloves, my people will notice. They know the real deal when they see it. You are supposed to be the best. Pathetic!"

Kurt says, "Mr President, we have made good progress. We are studying DNA samples from your assailant and the fluid to try to make sense of what is going on. May I take a DNA swab from you?"

Jack rounds on him. "No, you may not! You are treating me like a suspect! This is turning into a witch hunt!"

"With respect, Mr President, we need to isolate the contaminant from your own DNA."

"Why do people say 'with respect' when they don't fucking mean it? Get the hell out, all of you!"

Once clear of the Oval Office, Kingston motions Kurt to stop to confer, while the other brass move on.

"Why did you do risk upsetting him like that? Do you believe that crackpot Canadian already? I thought we needed a lot more evidence to get there."

"General, I am a scientist. I believe what the evidence tells me. And I don't have enough evidence yet to decide either way. As it happens I do have a DNA sample from him but not a high quality one and what it shows is pretty disturbing."

"Without actionable intel, we can't move against the president. His cabinet could invoke the 25th. But they and the Veep would have to be on board and they would need hard evidence. After the way he's treated the House they would love to impeach, but he controls the Senate. What do you need to make this solid, either way?"

"Time. And ideally a better DNA sample from the president – another water glass for example that he drank from that was wiped of DNA first. And I need the Canadian in case I need to ask him more questions. What's his name? Harper?"

"How much time? We have no idea what the consequences will be when it's obvious that he's an alien – or if he claims to be a human transformed to one. We can't, for example, risk a war with the aliens. They seem pathetic one on one but their weapons outmatch ours."

"As much as possible. At least a week."

"We need to deal with this before it is impossible for him

to hide it. Or finds his own way to turn it off, if he really is one of them. I have a safe house and the FBI will turn the Canadian over to me. I outrank them on national security. Good enough?"

"It will have to be. I'll get the kid to pack up my stuff."

* * * *

Kurt and Jamie are loading the last of their equipment into Kurt's car.

A marine marches toward them. "New orders, Sir! The president will not allow you to work outside the White House. You are to return immediately. Sir!"

"Like fuck he does. I have to do this work in a secure location and this one right now is not secure."

"I have orders to stop you." The marine reaches for his sidearm. Kurt moves in a blur, translating the marine's reach for his firearm to the marine landing on his face, Kurt's boot on his head, his gun in Kurt's hand.

"You go back to the president and let him know. I am a civilian and not under his orders."

The marine reaches for his firearm and Kurt shoves him away holding the weapon clear and points it slightly past the marine's head.

"Jamie. In the car now. Marine! You stay exactly where you are until we are out of sight."

Kurt jumps into the car and guns the engine. He tosses the marine's sidearm a good distance as they drive off.

Chapter 9

Car games

"No time to waste. Obviously stopping us at the gate has not reached the chain of command otherwise why send that idiot? Jamie, are you OK?"

"A bit shook up – not what happens in my day job. But I'm fine."

They clear the gate with no trouble and Kurt drives without drama. It is getting dark as they hit the public road.

"Kingston had better be right about the safe house."

"I hope so too. Is that car following us?" Jamie looks back to double-check.

"Not for long." Kurt times going through an intersection just before the light goes red. The other car follows resulting in honking and brakes squealing.

Kurt says, "Oh, crap. Now we know it's serious. No legit law enforcement would do that."

They round a corner and Kurt kills the lights and stops

at the side of the road. He gets out quickly; motions Jamie to follow and get down. The other car shoots past, brakes, backs up rapidly alongside and, without a word, the passenger rolls down his window and shoots up Kurt's car. The driver gets out, walks around the front of his car to Kurt's and finds himself face down, his own gun to his head.

The other occupant tries to get out but he is out of luck. Kurt's carefully-chosen interception point puts him near the assailants' passenger door. Kurt knees the door into his face. The driver uses the distraction to grab for his firearm and Kurt kicks him in the head. Neither attacker moves.

"Jamie, not sure if my car will go with so many holes in it. This one just has a bent door. Lucky they didn't shoot up the samples. Let's move our gear."

He and Jamie move fast. All is soon loaded in the second car and they move off.

Kurt drives without drama. "We can't take this car to the safe house. It could be tracked, they could pick it up on CCTV – who knows what assets they have… Let's take the metro and walk the rest of the way. Watch for cameras, make sure your face is obscured."

Chapter 10

Safe house

Harper is already in the safe house when they arrive. Outside, a marine patrols discretely. Kurt and Jamie confer.

Kurt says, "Not clear how much of government is working against us. Seems like they're a very makeshift operation."

"How safe is this house?"

"No reason not to trust Kingston. For now. But be ready to pack up and move fast. Key thing is, every move against us makes the Canadian's story more plausible." Kurt gestures at Harper.

"I just wonder at Jack's base. Are they endlessly gullible? Even without this, he disqualifies himself as presidential at least three times before lunch."

"Jamie, have you never had a relationship go seriously, abusively wrong?"

"No, not seriously, I mean I had break ups."

"Not like my friend Jane. Sticks with Jack despite all kinds of abuse. Denial is a powerful force."

"Ah, the other Jack. I wonder how much of that is the same force of nature. Fool me once, shame on you. Fool me twice, shame on me. Fool me every day, it's a cult."

"So... to work. Jamie, time for you to show off your lab skills to your professor."

Chapter 11

Breaking World News: BWN

The president is at the podium at a White House press conference. The press corps is there in numbers.

"Wendy Garcia, *New York Times*... I suppose you were first." Jack looks doubtful, but she does not hesitate.

"Mr President, is there any truth in the report that you were sprayed with a fluid from the aliens?"

"Why do I even bother taking a question from the failing *New York Times*? That is fake news and you know it! Fake news! Wendy Garcia, you are a disgrace to your profession! A disgrace! Enemy of the people!"

"Mr President, then why are you not using your usual expansive hand gestures?"

"Did I say you could have a follow up? Dana Ansell, BWN. You seem excited."

"Damn straight I am. How dare you call a journalist 'enemy of the people'? Countries like Saudi Arabia and Egypt detain journalists without trial, murder them and torture them. We..."

Jack is not at all fazed. "Enemy of the people! Saudis are wonderful. Buy so many weapons from us. So much money. Next! You! Not from Canada I hope?"

"No, Mr President, I am Elifas Kasingo, Namibian National Broadcaster."

"Ah, *Nambia*, I love Nambia, a very nice country. Causes no trouble at all. What is your question?"

"Are you aware of conflict between alien factions in the Canada refugee camp? Does your government have a response to that?"

Jack says, "Factions. Terrible thing. Where did they learn that from? So peaceful before. So peaceful."

"And your government's response?"

Jack says, "The time is long gone when America is the world's policeman. Let the Canadians work it out themselves. Behind my beautiful wall! Any Canadians here? Not like that terrible one I hope!"

Pandemonium. Numerous reporters shout questions like "what happened to him? Is he indicted?"

The president strides out.

*   *   *   *

The camera picks up the Canadian alien camp from a distance. Choppers are in the air and various USCS vehicles are parked aimlessly.

A generic anchor intones: "Here at the Canadian alien site, things have calmed down. Whatever factional battle was going on between the aliens seems to be over. We have a spokesperson for security contractor USCS, Captain Rivera. Captain, what can you tell us?"

"Yeah, things have cooled off. These bugs..."

"Excuse me captain, but is it company policy to call them that?"

"Sorry, no, ... these *aliens* have their own politics that we don't understand. Factions seem to be a new thing. Used to be just like an ant heap. No one in charge and not used to doing their own thing. Like the queen ant was missing, if you ask me."

"So do you mean they are starting to behave more like humans?"

"How do you mean?"

"More like individuals, vying for power for themselves and so on..."

"Yeah, I see what you mean." Rivera clams up. "You need to talk to our research people. I just do security."

*   *   *   *

The scene shifts to a PAFA rally with Jack at a podium amidst a sea of bright orange PAFA hats.

Jack yells: "Put America First Again! Yeah!"

And the crowd chants back: "PAFA! PAFA! PAFA!"

Jack gets into his stride. "The fake news media are telling crazy stories. Crazy! They are completely nuts! That reporter threw muddy water at me now I am not fit to be president! A total witch hunt!" He makes an expansive gesture with heavily gloved hands.

Jack: "A witch hunt! Lock them up!"

Crowd: "Lock them up! Lock them up! Lock them up!"

Jack: "Keep Canadian aliens out!"

Crowd: "Build the wall! Build the wall!"

Jack: "Who's going to pay?"

Crowd: "Canada! Canada!"

Zoom out: the video is embedded in Twitter. Tweets scroll past.

Jack fan @Jackfan: #BuildTheWall! Canada's the enemy!

The True Lib @deepStateBlue: Typical ever-Jacker.

Jack fan @Jackfan: A proud ever-Jacker.

The True Lib @deepStateBlue: You are all a bunch of Jackers if you ask me.

Jack fan @Jackfan: So disrespectful! No other president has ever been disrespected like this!

The True Lib @deepStateBlue: #Jackass
Literally EVERY previous Democratic
president has been disrespected more by
Republicans #JackerPresident

You took a coloured ribbon from out of the sky
And taught me how to use it as the years went by
To tie up all your problems and make them look neat
And then to sell them to the people in the street

Chapter 12

Safe house

In the safe house, Kurt and Jamie look up from their work of assembling lab gear as there is a loud thump in the background. Harper starts from his reverie.

The back door opens and Cy Campbell strides in, toting two impressive weapons, each glowing blue.

Kurt says, "What the fuck! This is a safe house. How did you get in here?"

"Safe from humans, perhaps."

Jamie looks shocked. "From humans...?" He stares at Campbell. "You mean you're..."

Kurt looks at Campbell intently. "... another disguised alien. Obviously. Jamie's not as slow as he looks."

Campbell motions to the door. "There is no time to argue. The president's faction has screwed up majorly and has no assets in the White House and no excuse to get one in now things are so locked down. But if I can track you here, so

can they, and your guards' weapons are no match for these."
He throws one at Harper who catches it. It goes dark as it
leaves Campbell's grasp and lights up blue as soon as Harper
touches it.

Harper stares at the weapon. "Now wait a minute. These
only work for aliens. The cure..."

Campbell says, "Still enough of our DNA in your system
to key to the weapon. Let's move!"

Harper freezes; it stays lit in his hands.

Kurt asks, "What of the marines outside?"

Campbell moves to the door, gesturing urgently. "Temporarily misdirected to the front yard. Come on, we need to
get out fast. Out the back!"

It's a strange, strange world we live in, Master Jack
You taught me all I know and I'll never look back
It's a very strange world and I thank you, Master Jack

Chapter 13

Breaking World News: BWN

We see the Canadian alien camp from a distance. The mothership overhead suddenly shoots upwards at speed. The camera tracks it but it's too fast and vanishes.

"Drama at the Canadian alien site. Just when the action seemed to be over, the mothership has vanished as we speak. Captain Rivera is with me again. Captain, what can you tell us?"

Rivera says, "Yeah... no. This is a big surprise. We were expecting them to load their people up before they left."

"Factional battles, previously unheard of. Now this. Is this a threat to humanity?"

"I am sorry –" Rivera shakes his head – "you will need to talk to my bosses. I only handle security."

"Jake: any thoughts? Are you picking up anything in the

studio?"

"Nothing to add. Stay tuned for this breaking story."

Aliens are milling aimlessly and there is no sign of active security in or around the camp. BWN switches to other news.

Chapter 14

Back yard and out

Out back is a dropship with an open hatch. Campbell ushers them in. Harper is last and on his way in turns and takes out a wing of the house in a blue flash.

The marine guard rounds a corner of the house, handgun at the ready. Kurt pulls Harper in as a round ricochets off the hatch. "What the fuck did you do that for? Don't you know what a decoy is?"

"Jesus fucking Christ! I didn't believe that thing would actually work."

They take off as the hatch closes. Blue flashes are visible on the ground below and machine guns respond. There are big yellow flashes and loud explosions. The marine, losing sight of the dropship, swings back to the front of the house.

As the dropship vanishes upwards, it's briefly rocked by a blue beam.

Campbell is at the controls. Flashes below remain visible

but none are close since the initial blue beam. They shoot upwards into the dark.

Kurt says, "You were not kidding about them finding us fast."

"They have the same tech as I do except they are using human wheels. We are going to the mothership where we have a proper lab and you can advise my people on human DNA."

"To do what?" asks Kurt, turning to Campbell who launches into a monologue.

"President faction's desperate to reverse the cure. We think we can stop him but it can't hurt to have your expertise as well.

"He has a few days before he can't hide it any more. We can't rely on keeping his faction out of the White House. I got in claiming to be an embassy-appointed lawyer. It's a matter of time before they think of a dodge. We need to prevent the cure from being undone.

"Once he can't deny it any more, we can take him out of there. But until then, any attempt to do so can be turned against us.

"Fortunately we control all the advanced tech and their numbers are small. From what we know so far, he's the only factionalist who's converted to look human. But we can't risk the possibility that we missed one or there's another traitor in our midst.

"We need to do all this without killing him so it doesn't look like assassination."

Kurt asks, "Don't you have ways to smoke out spies?"

"Factionalism is human stupidity. A few of us unfortunately learned that from you. We are not used to mistrust and betrayal in our ranks. Meantime all we can fall back on is making sure the cure keeps working on the president even if he does get help."

Jamie asks, "And you can do that?"

"Yes. But we need help with human DNA to counter anything they try."

There's another bright blue flash and Campbell does an evasive manoeuvre though it's not even a near miss.

Jamie looks at Kurt. "Is it OK to be scared?"

"Kid, it's dumb not to be scared. I got two purple hearts for being dumb. Don't let anyone tell you anything different. You get these things for being wounded, which is easy in a war – easier if you're stupid. After the second one, I realised that you aren't supposed to have PTSD already when you go into war and having no feelings is not a good thing. So I quit."

"PTSD before you started?"

"The classic story, why people join the French Foreign Legion. Girlfriend dumped me. Took it too hard."

"That guy's wife? Married to the other Jack…"

"Jane? No, she's Melissa's best friend. Jane helped me pick up the pieces after Mel dumped me. Then they both married jerks. Special forces seemed like a soft option after that."

After a short time in the air, the mothership looms large overhead.

Kurt stares. "Now wait… isn't that thing in Canada,

across the border from Nebraska?"

Campbell says, "Long story short... we need it here. Now. And moving it here is a lot faster than using the drop-ship to get there. So we can get to work in minutes, not hours. We have all the equipment we need and our top scientists on the mothership."

"So we won't need this then?" Jamie pulls a portable DNA sequencer out of his jacket pocket.

Kurt grins. "No harm having that. Too much equipment's better than too little."

Chapter 15

Mothership

Campbell obviously knows his way around the mothership and is known – there is no drama landing in it and exiting the dropship.

They run through corridors, Campbell in the lead, then Kurt, followed by Harper with Jamie at the rear, struggling to keep up. The corridors are suffused with a strange green light. There's weird plumbing along the ceilings and screens of odd shapes as well as holo displays showing alien text. They follow Campbell into a lab. Three alien scientists are there, puzzling over numerous weird-looking graphics displays. As in the corridor, some are screens and some are holograms.

Campbell addresses Kurt. "Our scientists will need help with your language. I can help some but I'm not a scientist."

"Tell us what they have now."

"Human mouth parts don't work for our language. So I

have to use writing." He sketches on a virtual display. Alien scientists respond with rapid-fire pings.

Harper listens intently. "Something about skin colour. I picked up some words in my alien camp days."

Campbell concurs. "Yes. They need to know which part of the human genome does skin colour."

"Not so simple." Kurt shakes his head. "There are lots of variables."

Jamie squints at Campbell. "I thought something was a bit off. You don't expect a turquoise tinge in human colouring."

Harper grins. "Yeah, but who's noticed that Jack's skin is orange and his hair is like plastic?"

Kurt gets back to business. "Can we access Internet from here?"

Campbell sketches again amidst acknowledgements from an alien scientist. "Yes. Let me get that set up, then I can leave you to it. I need to catch up on what we've found out about the factional plot. Perhaps Harper can help a bit with non-technical translation."

Frantic computer activity and discussion follows. Screen content and holograms move fast. Campbell does a lot of sketching and Harper fills in the odd gap, sometimes with comical malapropisms. Clearly, he is no scientist.

After a while, Campbell appears to be happy that communication is under control. "OK, that's the basics – be back shortly."

Jamie catches his attention. "One thing that's puzzling me. You have all these super weapons and it seems you can do interstellar travel. Yet you dumped most of your people on our unfriendly planet under unpleasant conditions."

Campbell pauses on his way out. "Multidimensional interstellar travel is difficult stuff. I am not an expert and don't have the human vocabulary to describe it. It takes a lot out of us and our equipment. That's why we need the DNA repair virus. This trip was supposed to be routine. But the transition was particularly bad and left our energy source depleted and damaged. We are not far from completing repairs and replenishing energy but would have been there a lot sooner without the complications of this stupid factionalism."

"So interstellar travel is routine for you?" asks Jamie.

"Compared with your space, travel, yes. We still do not undertake it lightly. We always plan on a stop at a habitable planet where we can repair and replenish. Some friendly, some not."

"And this one is…" Jamie realises that Campbell has gone "… not."

Chapter 16

Down to the ground

Jack is at the podium of yet another rally: a sea of bright orange PAFA hats extends as far as the eye (or camera) can see.

Jack is yelling. "Put America First Again! Yeah! PAFA! PAFA!"

Crowd chants: "PAFA! PAFA! PAFA!"

"The deep state is turning on me! Won't let my own friends into the White House!"

There's a dismayed buzz from the audience then: "LOCK THEM UP! LOCK THEM UP!"

"But what they don't know is... YOU ARE ALL MY FRIENDS!"

Jack pauses and is gratified by the crowd. "BUILD THE WALL! BUILD THE WALL!" There's a hint of confusion in the tone even if it is loud.

Jack roars: "When I give the word, WILL YOU ALL

STORM THE WHITE HOUSE? Show them who's boss in America!" This wins a huge answering roar from the crowd.

The camera pans over the angry crowd, almost frothing at the mouth. Then back to Jack, basking in adulation.

Visualize: zoom out and the video is embedded in Twitter. Tweets scroll past.

Jack fan @Jackfan: #DeepState exposed! Be ready to #stormWhiteHouse!

The True Lib @deepStateBlue: Are you mad? Jack is clearly unhinged. Or an alien. Or both!

Jack fan @Jackfan: PAFA! PAFA! The greatest president ever. Putting America First!

The True Lib @deepStateBlue: Putting aliens first, more like!

Jack fan @Jackfan: Libtards, do anything to take down best president ever. #PAFA!

Now zoom back into the video. Jack says contemplatively, his tone swinging up and down, "When I give the word! They will see." The crowd is calming a bit, looking around, as if not able to believe where they are going with this.

Jack gets back on form. "Drain the swamp! Drain the swamp! PAFA! LOCK THEM UP!"

The crowd lifts again: "PAFA! PAFA! LOCK THEM UP! LOCK THEM UP!" – the two chants merge into a general hubbub.

Chapter 17

Mothership

Campbell is back. The scientists and humans are so engrossed that no one pays attention to him until he speaks. "You guys making progress?"

Jamie says, "I think so. We found a common language for DNA sequences and are getting closer. We are comparing a sample from me and from the Canadian, and making some sense of each other's notation."

"Good."

Kurt looks up from his work. "You didn't explain where we're going with this exactly."

"Just a starting point."

"Why would you need that to stop the presidential faction?" Jamie looks puzzled.

"We need a quicker way to understand how our virus interacts with human DNA. We can work it on general principles but it would be faster if we knew how things encode.

This virus was never intended for this exact purpose. It was engineered to repair damaged DNA in our species and related species. Somehow, despite appearances, humans are close enough to us for this – uh – repair to work this way and it was a relatively easy process for the rebel faction to engineer a variant to do the reverse once we had the trick.

"However, we do not have details of how the reverse mechanism plays out in this scenario because we have not previously studied human DNA, and they erased their research before they left."

"Reverse? The cure?" asks Harper.

"No, the reverse-species switch. Us to human. All they failed to destroy was one dose of their virus – I volunteered to test it. The cure is simpler: if you kill the virus, the body steadily reverts to type. It's designed that way in case the virus causes an adverse effect when used as designed. The cure is a very simple but very specific low-dose anti-viral. Easy when you designed the virus yourself.

"Fortunately, the variant that makes one of us look human also responds to the cure, as discovered by this man." He points to Harper.

"Yeah, I think I get it. And what about my old friends, Antonio and Juan? Is your faction in touch with them?"

A flash of anger crosses Campbell's face, the effect rendered comical in a swirl between red and turquoise. "Faction? We are not a faction. We want to get rid of all factions. Back to how we were before humans confused us. Unity. Power. One species, one goal."

"And humans?" Kurt asks.

"We have the tech for you to join us, discovered by accident by your friend here." He points to Harper. "Before he was accidentally infected, we didn't realize that a cross-species switch was possible. Now we know, it has opened a whole new field of genomics editing. So we would like representatives from your group to do the species switch too. That should be a start to cross-species cooperation in a way we could not envisage before.

"That or we make sure you have no way to threaten us.

"But we are not interested in your factional friends. That is not our way. From zero factions to two is the wrong trend. We need to get back to zero."

Kurt returns to the main point. "And the president?"

"There's a new complication. I just found out that his faction made a total of six human conversions before we were onto them and they escaped. Unfortunately, before we knew what they looked like. Without knowing who the other five are and what they are up to, I fear our plan of allowing the president to become obviously alien is not enough. We need other options."

"And their skin colour...?" Jamie asks. "You and the president are both a little – uh – odd if you don't mind me saying."

"Since we can't track down the others, who are also certainly also a bit off-colour so to speak, I am guessing they use a lot of make up."

"How –" Kurt asks – "did they hatch the plot to get elected as our president?"

"It started when we were studying human psychology

and ran into a study that showed only five percent of scams are ever reported. Humans are so easy to manipulate. Persuade them to believe something that makes no sense and they can't back out because they don't want to admit they're fools. Just like that, you have control of your planet's only superpower."

"So you decided to use this?"

"No – most of us just marvelled at how stupid humans are. Unfortunately, we stopped at seeing that as a point of superiority of our culture. A small group hatched this plot and were overruled. Next thing we knew, they had taken over a lab and now we discover that they have infiltrated six fake humans into your society. Even if it was something we would do, we didn't expect it to work. I mean, really, a global superpower with your planet's best science and technology, that easy to take over?"

"Never underestimate the power of human stupidity." Kurt looks grim.

Jamie adds, "So Jack makes sure he says at least 5 stupidly untrue things before breakfast so his base have even more reason to find it hard to admit they're fools. Adds new meaning to neocon."

Campbell looks puzzled. "To what?"

"Neocon: it usually means a new kind of conservative. Jack is a new kind of *con*. His superpower. Mass delusion on a scale never seen before."

"And us? The plan is...?" Kurt asks.

"You have useful knowledge. We can use you. If you want to join us, good. If not, we will make sure you do not interfere. You have to decide: this can be the starting point of humanity joining our alliance. Unity..."

"Yeah, I got the memo: ... Power. One species, one goal."

"It is not just this planet. We are allied with numerous other species, who join our unity, not by conquest... but the Jack faction is forcing our hand. Maybe for the good: we now have the tech for even closer unity."

Harper is not looking so happy. "Hey, wait a minute..."

Kurt butts in. "OK, thanks, Cy, or whatever your name is. We need time to think. Can you give us a few minutes?" He glances around at the alien scientists. "With a bit of privacy. Your people may have picked up a little English."

"Sure, but we need to find out a lot more about human DNA. So not a lot of time. I will post a guard who definitely does not understand your language."

He gestures to his scientists to leave with him. A guard shows up with one of the impressive alien weapons.

I saw right through the way you started teachin' me now
So some day soon you could get to use me somehow
I thank you very much and though you've been very kind
But I'd better move along before you change my mind

Chapter 18

Breaking World News: BWN

The president is yet again at a press conference podium. The press corps is there in tumult. He gives every appearance of gloating at their anxiousness to get in a question and picks one apparently at random.

It's Garcia. "Mr President, is there any truth in the report that there was a firefight involving alien weapons and a dropship right here in Washington DC?"

Jack: "Oh no! The failing *New York Times* again. That is fake news! Fake news! Wendy Garcia, you are a..."

Garcia: "I know, a disgrace to my profession. Nonetheless there are credible reports..."

Jack: "No there are not! Fake news. Enemy of the people! Give back the mike! I did not offer a follow up!"

Zoom out: the video is embedded in Twitter. Tweets

scroll past.

Jack fan @Jackfan: #FakeNews!
#FailingNewYorkTimes!
#EnemyOfThePeople!

The True Lib @deepStateBlue: Well, Fox
News reports it too.

Jack fan @Jackfan: You believe the
lying fake news?

The True Lib @deepStateBlue: Right, so
Fox is the new Fake.

Jack fan @Jackfan: #PAFA! Libtards!

Chapter 19

Mothership again

Kurt opens the conversation once he's sure Campbell and his scientists are out of earshot. "Apologies for shutting you up, Harper. We don't have a lot of time to think. We are being pushed to make a choice that is really for all humanity. It is not our choice to make on our own. Agreed?"

The others nod grimly.

"One thing I don't get. Why not just infect all humans with this virus?"

"Think it through, Jamie. It's obviously not highly infectious, otherwise our friend here would have taken more with him. He got a lot of it splashed in his face. So it needs a high dose, direct contact.

"Say they re-engineer it to be more contagious. How do viruses spread fastest? Generally, respiratory spread. But we know how to contain a respiratory virus. WHO and CDC just need to dust off their playbooks. And what does it buy them? Harper, is it not true that simply changing to alien mouth parts stops you speaking like a human but does not teach you the alien language?"

"Yeah. I knew the lingo from working with them but it still took time to learn to talk it myself."

"And anyway," Jamie adds, looking a bit foolish, "if they did that, it would give us an army capable of stealing and using their tech."

Kurt brings the conversation back to the here and now. "We don't have a lot to work with. We're on an alien space ship with no idea how the thing flies. We are surrounded by alien super weapons that only one of us can use. We know roughly where the dropship is but no one here has flown one before."

Harper volunteers, "Well, actually, I did before. Remember?"

Jamie interjects, "And crashed."

"The time I was shot down, yes. It is not so hard to fly. It was no problem the second time when I went to get the cure from Antonio."

"Could you do that again? Wouldn't it be better if I flew it?" Kurt asks. "I've flown pretty much everything known to humanity."

"Maybe but it seems I can still use alien stuff. No 'on' switch, it just goes if you are one of them. Not at all if you are not. I handled one of those weapons before I was infected and it didn't even light up."

Kurt nods. "Main point is we agree: we are not entitled to decide the future of the human race. I need to get back to people I trust. General Kingston for a start.

"We can work out flying the thing if we get that far. Are we agreed, we escape?"

Grim nods all round.

"I think so." Jamie turns to Harper. "What was it like being one of them?"

"Weird. Not what I wanted to be. Never in my own skin. But amazing weapons. Like super powers."

"OK, so we agree, we are not volunteering." With no further ado, Kurt taps the guard on a shoulder. The guard pings rapidly at him and reaches for its weapon. Kurt knees it in the groin, then shouts in pain and grabs his knee. The guard pings rapid-fire.

Harper uses the distraction to snatch its weapon and it pings even more as he levels it.

Harper says, "Yeah, I do actually understand your language, thanks. Canada camp. Remember that?"

The alien casually reaches for the weapon, pinging ferociously. Harper lets rip with a beam of blue fire; the alien vapourises.

"And, actually, you are wrong, I can use your weapon." Harper eyes out the spot where the alien used to be.

He adds, "Apology accepted."

Kurt moves with urgency. "Let's go. No time for pleasantries. To the dropship bay." He grabs Jamie who is not moving except to stuff things in pockets. Jamie unfreezes and runs.

Kurt produces his own sidearm. "Lucky they think we are so pathetic that they didn't take this."

Harper is laughing as he runs; Kurt is slightly hobbling and not laughing.

Kurt ignores the mirth. "Harper, you used to be one of these things. Which parts are vulnerable?"

"Like an insect, hard on the outside though they do actually have a skeleton inside as well. A bullet will get through but not so much a knee. I never did actually try to hurt myself but I imagine a gun would stop them as much as it would stop one of us."

In the reverse of the run to the lab, fortunately a relatively straightforward route, they make good progress until about halfway, when an alien twigs that there is a problem and pings furiously.

Kurt says, "What's it saying, Harper?"

"Something like stop or I shoot."

"Use that thing! No time to argue."

Kurt applies blue fire. The alien disappears and others scatter for cover as they run. Aliens are getting more organized and start firing back. They dodge as Harper fires back clumsily but the weapon seems to know what to do. Shortly, only two aliens are still following but seem more capable than the rest. The humans round a corner, just missed by blue beams.

Kurt points down the next corridor. "Run! Let me deal with this." He jumps cat-like into ceiling plumbing, sidearm at the ready, just before the aliens appear, gets them both rapid-fire, drops to the floor, and catches the others.

Kurt calls out, "Come on! Nearly there."

More aliens appear further behind. Just as they reach the

dropship, Harper's alien gun stutters into rapid slowing clicks
– sounds reminiscent of a car's starter motor dying when the
battery is on the way out. Kurt uses his sidearm on the last
two aliens in sight.

Kurt yells: "Quick! Into the dropship! I just hope you
really can work this."

Harper dashes in and Kurt pushes Jamie, taking another
shot as they get inside. The dropship lurches to life. Kurt
shoots a new alien whose weapon clatters into the dropship.
The hatch closes. The dropship moves just in time to avoid
a blue blast. It bounces off the walls as it heads for the open
bay, glances off the lip and into clear air.

Kurt shakes his head. "Either that was some impressive
evasive manoeuvres or. . ."

It's a strange, strange world we live in, Master Jack
You know how I feel as if I'll never come back
It's a very strange world and I thank you, Master Jack

Chapter 20

Breaking World News: BWN

About ten people with placards such as

STORM THE WHITE HOUSE

FREE ACCESS TO OUR PRESIDENT

PAFA

DOWN WITH DEEP STATE

are milling around outside the White House, which is visible in the distance.

They are chanting slogans like "PAFA" (which is only a slogan to the initiates), "No deep state!", "Jack third term!"

Two anchors alternate commentary.

"A small crowd has appeared outside the White House. They appear to have anticipated the call to storm the White House."

"At least they have not done something stupid like show up armed."

"Nonetheless, Will, a worrying development as the president appears to be at odds with his own Secret Service detail."

Chapter 21

Dropship drops

Kurt holds onto anything that provides a handhold. "Harper! You said you could fly this thing!"

"I didn't say I was expert. You try."

Kurt grabs the controls. They do not respond.

"Damn! We have to rely on you. We went pretty much straight up so if you can take us roughly straight down, we should not be very far off places I know."

The dropship is going down far from smoothly. Kurt looks out for landmarks.

Jamie hefts the alien weapon that landed inside from the last attacker. "Some alien blood on it – another DNA sample."

Kurt yells, "Watch what you do with that thing!"

Harper smiles. "It will do nothing unless I touch it. Even the dead one shows a blue light if I touch it."

He demonstrates on the dead one and reaches for the

other one, presumably still charged.

Kurt says, "OK, OK. I believe you. No need to test it when we want this bucket to land in one piece." The bouncing plummet continues.

"See that structure down there? Pentagon!"

"What do you mean like... five sides?"

Kurt says, "No! Well, yes, I mean *The* Pentagon. Don't they teach you anything in Canada?"

"Apologies. I actually grew up in the United States."

Kurt eyerolls. "Take us down near there, not too close because it has serious defenses."

"OK, I'll do my best."

The dropship comes to a crashing halt right up against The Pentagon. Troops appear in numbers, guns at the ready, flanked by armoured vehicles with seriously big guns.

Kurt says, "If that is your best, I hate to see your worst. Open the hatch and let's await orders from them."

A tall figure in fatigues marches to the front of the troops. Kingston. "You! On the alien craft! Come out peacefully with no weapons! Hands visible!"

"General! Kurt Lowell here! We escaped from the alien mothership. We are no threat."

Kurt emerges, hands facing the troops. "Jamie, Harper! Out! same way as me."

They all emerge.

Kingston says, "Anyone else on the craft, Colonel?"

"No, just us. There is an alien weapon there but the power seems to be exhausted. We have another on the craft that we didn't discharge yet, probably still usable. But only by an alien or our friend Harper, who's been contaminated with alien DNA. I left my sidearm inside as well."

Kingston addresses the troops. "All right, stand down. You two! Into the craft with us."

He points at two grunts, and gestures to Kurt. They all emerge shortly with the two alien weapons and Kurt is re-holstering his own. The two alien weapons are wrapped up and gingerly removed by a soldier. All the while, they do not light up.

Chapter 22

Breaking World News: BWN

We alternate between two anchors again.

"Amateur footage of the alien dropship almost crashing into The Pentagon is not clear but it appears that only humans were escorted out of the craft. Jake, does this mean there really are aliens disguised as humans?"

"Will, you mean as alleged about President Jack? At this point, we can only speculate. Unfortunately we have no footage showing a clear view of any of the people. Or possibly aliens. Escorted away by the military."

"Until we can can get confirmation from The Pentagon, we cannot be sure."

"What does this say about the president's earlier denial of a dropship landing in DC?"

"Notch another onto the count of lies. Are you keeping

up?"

Grainy footage of the dropship's dramatic landing follows, followed in short order by rapid deployment of the military. Finally, the amateur footage wobbles to three figures being hustled away, backs to camera.

Zoom out: the video is once again embedded in Twitter. Tweets flow thick and fast, though some thicker than others.

Jack fan @Jackfan: #DeepState plot! Trying to fool us into believing president is an alien!

The True Lib @deepStateBlue: So what if he's human? Let's say he is. He's human. A very damaged human.

Jack fan @Jackfan: You believe the lying fake news? Best president ever. Witch hunt!

The True Lib @deepStateBlue: Most dysfunctional president ever, more like. And #Jack lied about a dropship in DC before.

Jack fan @Jackfan: #PAFA! That wasn't the same thing!

The True Lib @deepStateBlue: Damn straight! He hasn't had time to lie about this one yet. #Jackass

Chapter 23

Pentagon: inside

Harper, Jamie and Kurt sit facing Kingston in an office in The Pentagon. Kingston sums up. "OK, so it's good news that the aliens only have one asset in the White House. Bad news: it's the president."

Kurt nods grimly. "The challenge is how to keep it that way. We need at least a week of intensive lab time even with what we know to figure out a test for alien DNA. We still only have the one compromised sample of the president. We could also work with Harper's DNA and we have an alien sample on the other weapon. But it's not clear if the Jack sample will help in screening for more aliens until we do more work on it. Our pocket sequencers can do basic stuff, but we could end up needing something more complex like PCR – the lab tech they use to test for flu and the like.

"In the meantime if we miss another disguised alien, they could get access to the president to reinfect him – and we don't even know if that's possible."

Kingston looks troubled. "You mean we have no way to stop another disguised alien from accessing the president until you come up with some new test, and you don't know how long that will take?"

"But we do have another test." Jamie looks thoughtful. "The weapon. It only lights up on contact with alien DNA."

"And blows away anything we can use against it. No thanks." Kingston looks more than a little dismissive.

Kurt intervenes. "The kid's got a point. We have one that's discharged, can't be fired. But it still lights up on alien touch. Anyone the president wants let into his inner circle gets shown the weapon, manoeuvred into touching it."

Kingston says, "OK, that could work, at least to buy us a few days."

*   *   *   *

Jack is at a podium, amidst yet another sea of bright orange PAFA hats. This has to be another rally. Does he not have an actual job?

Jack yells: "PAFA! PAFA! Lock them up!"

Crowd chants: "PAFA! PAFA! PAFA!"

Jack: "Those lying liberals want to see my birth certificate! Who do they think they are? No other president was EVER ASKED FOR THAT!"

Crowd: "Lock them up! Lock them up!"

Jack: "Well, here is my birth certificate!" He produces a colourful sheet of paper to loud cheers.

We are back in the BWN studio, with the usual quota of two alternating anchors.

"Jake, hold up a minute and let's zoom in on that piece of paper."

The image focuses into a circle around Jack's hand, considerably enlarged.

"It looks like he just held up a Chick-fil-A take-out menu and claimed it's his birth certificate. Back to live action. This should be interesting."

The picture goes back to the rally, cheers subsiding.

Jack declaims with great drama, "Let me tell you how much I care about showing them my birth certificate."

He holds it up in a gloved hand and sets the paper on fire. The crowd erupts. The camera zooms in on him. His neck looks a little grey.

The video is embedded in Twitter. Tweets scroll past once again.

Jack fan @Jackfan: #DeepState exposed! Be ready to #stormWhiteHouse!

The True Lib @deepStateBlue: You said that before. Now turns out he's a son of a Chick-fil-A.

Jack fan @Jackfan: You believe the lying fake news? That was for sure his

birth certificate! Photoshopped! Best
president ever.

The True Lib @deepStateBlue: Best take
out menu, more like!

Jack fan @Jackfan: #PAFA!

The True Lib @deepStateBlue: What's
that? Alien for son of a chicken? Or
son of a #Jackass?

Chapter 24

White House checkpoint

Kurt and Kingston are at a White House checkpoint with two marines. A car is stopped; inside is a very fat man in a suit that is obviously outside the pay grade of everyone else present. He is arguing vociferously with one of the marines as Kingston approaches and intervenes, since the marine is obviously getting nowhere.

"I am sorry sir, everyone gets searched at this checkpoint. The fact that a general is here should make it clear how seriously we take the security of the president. Please get out of the car, or we will turn you away."

The fat man proffers a document. "I am Rudi Corleone, the president's new counsel. Read this. It is a letter from the president demanding immediate access and a White House pass. The paperwork for that should all be done."

Kingston says, "Sir, that is all in order. We have the paperwork. Nonetheless, we must go through all security checks. Marines, check the car." Corleone gets out grudgingly and opens the trunk.

The marines scan the car with various devices including a mirror to check underneath and open all doors and interior compartments.

Kingston approaches Corleone as he is about to re-enter his car. "One final thing. Have you seen one of these before?" Kurt hands Corleone the discharged weapon.

Corleone looks at it in trepidation. "What? Of course not. I am a lawyer, not a weapons expert." He handles the weapon indelicately and nothing lights up. He passes it back.

Kingston passes it to Kurt. "Thank you, just a routine check. Marines, if you are happy we can let him through. Sir, please accept my apologies but we *will* have to search your car again next time you drive in."

Corleone gets into the car angrily and drives off. Kurt looks down the road, brandishing the weapon.

Chapter 25

Oval Office

Jack is pacing in front of the Resolute Desk. Corleone is seated, his eyes following Jack's every move.

Jack stops and fixes his visitor with a glare. "They did what?"

"Intimidation, sir. Rank intimidation. What did they mean by passing me that grotesque weapon?"

"Did they not explain?"

"They said just a routine check."

"A check! How dare they? I am their commander in chief. How dare they check my people?"

"Sir, while I agree with you, they do have authority over your safety. On national security matters, the president generally does not interfere with operational..."

"I brought you in because you are a fighter! Are you throwing in the towel already?"

"No, sir. I am just pointing out the norm. I am here for

you because you are not the norm." Corleone is quick on his feet for someone who's sitting down. And so fat.

Jack says, "Now you're talking. Tell me what I can do about this!"

"They can control access to the White House but they can't control who you see anywhere else, other than routine security screening. Organize a public event, a business meeting, whatever it takes to see whoever you need to without going through them."

"Excellent! Stupid suspicion that I'm an alien. You don't believe that do you?"

"Sir, it is not up to me to have an opinion on that. The people I work for are happy with the results and that's what counts.

"You keep people distracted with culture wars while doing the real things that matter. Undoing obstacles to profits. Environmental regulation down the plughole. A record number of business-friendly Supreme Court justices. They couldn't be happier."

You taught me all the things the way you'd like them to be
But I'd like to see if other people agree
It's all very interesting the way you disguise
But I'd like to see the world through my own eyes

Chapter 26

White House checkpoint

Mannon, Kurt, Kingston and Jamie confer in the guard hut at the White House checkpoint where Corleone entered. Outside, there's a brief commotion.

A Marine approaches Kurt. "Sir, there is someone demanding to see the colonel, uh, professor."

"Who?" Kurt asks.

"Won't say, says it's personal."

Kurt exits and sees Jane at the boom.

"Jane! What are you doing here?"

"You were pretty damn conspicuous waving that alien weapon at the cameras. Right here, which is why I'm right here. There's something I really want to tell you and you are not picking up your phone."

'What? Something urgent?"

"I want you to be the first to know. I walked out on Jack. Thanks to you."

"Wow. I didn't expect that. Sorry, can't talk now. Coffee? I will check my phone when things are quieter."

Jane turns reluctantly back to her car. "I will message you."

"I count on it."

Back inside, Kurt says, "Pretty sure the cameras got a good view of the weapon. If Jane saw it, that's a good sign. Any alien assets out there will know what we are up to."

Kingston grimaces. "But it troubles me that they have not tried to get another asset into the White House. You say they have six. That's Jack and five more. Mannon, has the FBI dug up anything more?"

"No. We have done extensive background checks on Jack and all his known associates. He is the only one where there are gaps in the record. He was well known up to college, dropped out of sight for a few decades then resurfaced."

Kurt adds, "Classic identity theft: find someone who's disappeared without trace and take over their identity."

Kingston nods. "Yup. Also explains the weird lapses in his memory about his own past. But no one else...?"

Jamie looks thoughtful. "Maybe we're looking in the wrong place. Supreme Court nominations. There was a vacancy when he took office and two conservative judges retired soon after. Then a liberal judge died conveniently. He already appointed four judges before the midterms. My girlfriend got me fired up over this: the first election when I was seriously involved."

Kurt says, "And another nomination is before the Senate right now. Kernighan. Agent Mannon, what do you think?"

"Of course! All of his four prior nominees as well as Kernighan have very skimpy backgrounds. But we had no reason to do a deep background on any of them."

"And they all got terribly negative reviews on everything except very right-wing judgements. Which is where I got involved, thanks to Karen."

Kingston takes over the conversation forcefully. "Jamie, great idea but we don't need more background from you. Agent, how fast could the FBI do detailed backgrounds on the first four and the new nominee?"

Mannon says, "Comprehensive: at least a week. But we already have some background on the others and did some routine checks on Kernighan. Very discrete of course because no one asked us."

"I fear we don't have a week," adds Jamie. "The Republican majority is close to pushing Kernighan through. Once that's done, we have to figure out how to unseat a Supreme Court Justice, which has to be a whole lot harder, if I understand correctly from Karen, than stopping it now."

"There is another way. We have a test." Kurt hefts the alien weapon.

Mannon looks quizzical. "How does that help?"

But Kingston gets it and elaborates on the plot before Kurt or Jamie can get in a word. "Fake a security scare, clear the hearing. In the chaos, make sure Kernighan comes in contact with the weapon. Did I understand that touching it anywhere makes it light up, Lowell?"

"One hundred percent. And no risk, it can't fire. Let's stop wasting our time here. Mannon, can you organize some reliable backup?"

"Absolutely."

Kingston adds, "Strictly need-to-know. We can't risk word of this ploy getting to the hearing ahead of us."

Chapter 27

Senate confirmation hearing

Dozens of protesters mill around amidst heavy security. They parade placards like

HANDS OFF ROE v. WADE

CORPORATIONS AREN'T PEOPLE

One of them is Karen, Jamie's girlfriend.

Mannon, Kurt, Kingston and Jamie push for the entrance with a large security contingent. Protesters shout angrily.

Kurt wields a large tote bag as if to add emphasis to his words. "We are not here to violate your rights. Do keep protesting. But we have a security alert and have to intervene to ensure everyone's safety."

Karen yells, "The only security concern is that person or thing in the White House and what he or it is doing to our rights!"

Then she catches sight of Jamie. "Jamie Curtis! What the hell are *you* doing with the law? And why are you not returning my calls? You should be here with me!"

Jamie pulls out his phone. "Oh, crap. I guess there was no signal on the mothership..."

"Mothership? Was that you?"

Kurt breaks in. "You know each other. Great. Jamie, you stay back here and explain to your friends what's going on. We have no time to waste."

"Everything?"

"Mothership. What is going on now once it unfolds. Time we stopped worrying about secrets."

A Democratic Senator is quizzing the nominee as Mannon, Kurt, Kingston and half a dozen FBI agents burst into the hearing. "Judge, there are a few things I do not understand about your track record. In fact, you can barely say you *do* have a track record."

Mannon leads with his ID. "Senators, apologies. Agent Mannon, FBI. We have had a security alert. We will have to clear the room. Since there is a big crush of protesters outside, we will have to take it one at a time."

The Republican chair bangs his gavel. "Is there nothing the left won't stoop to?"

Mannon gives every appearance of obsequious apology but somehow not meaning it. "Senator, we do not have any suspects and are not sure if the threat is credible, but we must act on it. Now if you please, one at a time."

The first five senators exit when Kernighan starts to move. Kurt moves towards him, grabs his hand and pulls the alien weapon out of the bag. Kernighan touches it – it lights up.

Kernighan grabs the weapon and roars: "Stupid humans! I'll kill you all!"

A shot rings out, fired by one of Mannon's agents. The alien weapon clatters to the floor and Kernighan's chest displays a growing red patch. His eyes roll up and he collapses amidst pandemonium.

Mannon checks for a pulse and finds none.

He turns to the shooter. "Dammit agent, we wanted him alive."

Mannon abandons feeling for a pulse and holds up fingers in surprise. On his fingers, there is something that looks like makeup and the skin where the makeup has come away looks blue-grey.

The agent apologises unapologetically. "Sorry, sir. I've seen what those alien weapons can do. Everyone in this room would've been dead in less than a minute."

"Agent, that weapon is discharged, not enough power left to shoot. But if an alien or someone contaminated with alien DNA touches it, it lights up even though it can't fire."

"Christ. Why didn't anyone tell us?"

Kurt eyerolls. "When need to know fails..."

Mannon makes do with a headshake. "What a goddam mess."

"I think you will find this time it is not just a matter of a lot of paperwork," Kurt adds, a little unnecessarily.

Chapter 28

Breaking World News: BWN

We are back to our two-anchor act on BWN.

"Jake, further evidence of aliens disguised as humans. What will Jack supporters make of this?"

"The same thing as they make of everything else. Fake news, deep state plots, denial of the obvious. And we're all enemies of the people. Some of whom are not actually people."

Zoom out: the video is embedded in Twitter. Tweets scroll past.

Jack fan @Jackfan: #DeepState plot! Trying to fool us into believing president is an alien! Now this! Murderers!

The True Lib @deepStateBlue: You heard him saying stupid humans and threatening to kill everyone. And that alien gun thing lit up. Only aliens can use alien tech.

Jack fan @Jackfan: You believe the lying fake news? Witch hunt! #EnemeyOfThePeople

---

The True Lib @deepStateBlue: Seems they found a witch.

Jack fan @Jackfan: #PAFA! Best president ever! #Jack third term!

The True Lib @deepStateBlue: For anti-choice you sure are keen to carry that thing to term.

BWN without further ado takes us to yet another PAFA rally, the usual scene with Jack at the podium surrounded by a sea of bright orange PAFA hats.

    Jack: "Deep state plot! Murderers! Lock them up!"
    Crowd: "PAFA! PAFA! PAFA!"
    Jack: "Best judge ever! They have no answers!"

Crowd: "Lock them up! Lock them up!"

Jack: "Remember my call to storm the White House!"

Crowd: "Lock them up! Lock them up! PAFA! PAFA!"

Jack: "I am the best president ever, a stable genius!"

Crowd: "PAFA! PAFA! PAFA!"

Somehow the crowd is not picking up the change of tone and the chants have a ring of same old, same old. "Lock them up! Lock them up! PAFA! PAFA!"

Jack roars, apparently trying to up the enthusiasm, "I know you will always have my back! And furthermore... PING PING PING PING PING!"

The crowd goes crazy.

Outside the PAFA Rally, PAFA-hats unable to make the cut for the stadium are milling around.

An interviewer addresses a random PAFA-hat. "As a Jack supporter, what do you make of the way he started pinging like an alien?"

PAFA-hat: "Hahahaha – totally owned the libs. They can accuse him of being an alien all they want but we know he's one of us."

Interviewer: "In what way do you relate to him? Even if he is not an alien, are you a billionaire?"

PAFA-hat: "Hahahaha – I am a temporarily inconvenienced billionaire. With his great policies, I will soon be super rich."

Interviewer: "Which of his policies will do that for you?"

PAFA-hat: "All of them. They are all good."

Interviewer: "Including tax cuts for the rich and millions losing their health insurance?"

PAFA-hat: "I didn't lose *my* health insurance."

Interviewer: "And you don't care that the last person he nominated to the Supreme Court has alien DNA? And the president can only ping as if he's an alien?"

PAFA-hat: "Fake news! Why am I even talking to you? Deep-state assassination!"

Chapter 29

University lab

Kurt, Jamie and Karen are watching BWN.

Kurt states the obvious. "Well, so much for the aliens' race to get him out before it gets obvious. That's if Campbell actually represents those in charge."

Karen looks grim. "I said this was a cult before. Now there's no doubt. Even though he's clearly an alien, they support him as if nothing's happening."

Jamie looks up. "Yeah, I'm just checking Jack's fan club tweets. The usual memes: fake news, deep state plot. And listen to this: *Jack totally owned the libs*. Prof, I don't know if you are up with social media."

"I'm not that old. I know that 'owned' has a social-media meaning. But Jack has total ownership of *them*."

Jamie keeps reading. "And this tops them all: *Jack third term*. Karen, he..."

"... hasn't even finished the first one. Let alone amending the constitution to do away with term limits."

"Karen, like we always say. Totally a cult of wacky conspiracy theories."

"Yet there is a conspiracy in plain sight. An alien has taken over the White House."

"I wonder what Cy is making of this."

Karen is puzzled. "Who?"

"Cy Campbell. The alien we last saw on the mothership."

"Ah. The turquoise. I wonder if his faction lost." Karen adds, "Oops, that sounded vaguely racist. Or should that be speciest? Saying something like that is so not me."

Kurt ignores her embarrassment. "Good question. I guess we would otherwise have heard from his totally not a faction faction by now if they really are on the winning side. The aliens do not seem too fazed about us escaping – after Campbell said he would make sure we didn't interfere."

Jamie asks, "We aren't, are we?"

"Interfering with what?" Karen fires back. "Do any of us know what is actually going on?"

Chapter 30

Oval Office

Jack and Corleone are alone in the Oval Office, with Jack behind the Resolute for once – and uncharacteristically silent. He passes Corleone a note.

"Sir, I am sorry about your voice. This changes nothing – allegations will not hurt you and in fact you continue to dominate the news cycle."

Another note.

"I appreciate that you like to reach out to your people but really, do they actually listen to anything you say?"

Note.

"Where will we find a translator? Do you mean those sounds are the actual alien language?"

Note.

"Well, I am not a linguist but if you think someone from the Canadian alien camp..."

Jack nods vigorously.

"I will talk to the FBI about clearance."

Note.

Corleone nods appreciatively. "Right, I see you have this all worked through. If the translator is a security contractor over there, this should be a formality."

Chapter 31

White House checkpoint

Kurt and Kingston are back at their familiar White House checkpoint but without Mannon, who's tied up in paperwork.

A crowd of about 20 PAFA-hats carrying a highly visible array of weapons approaches. Kingston walks out to them calmly. "Good day gentlemen. I will not belabour the fact that you are breaking any number of laws arriving armed in that fashion. Could you state your business?"

A random PAFA-hat says, "We're heeding the president's call to storm the White House."

Kingston smiles engagingly. "Well, gentlemen. Storm away. Far be it for me to intervene. But I should point out that people further down the road have much heavier weapons than you and none of you will be likely to get out alive."

Kingston turns his back and walks into the checkpoint building.

A guard confronts Kingston. "Sir, aren't you going to

stop them? DC is not open carry and approaching the White House armed..."

Kingston turns to Kurt. "I am a soldier. Colonel, you've done four tours in Afghanistan. Have I judged the situation correctly?"

Kurt starts protesting. "How many times...? It's professor... Sir, you are absolutely right. Millions were told to show up and this little rabble do not have the safety in numbers they expected. Leave the realization that they are making fools of themselves to sink in and they will slink off home."

"And if we do intervene with force...?"

"It was bad enough when that fake human judge was killed. This lot mean nothing unless they are harmed. Then they become big news. Twenty people showing up? It shows up Jack's call to storm the White House. There's plenty of cameras watching so best it stays as 'fizzled out'."

The phone rings and the guard answers. "General, sir, it's for you."

Kingston takes the phone. "Yes, sir. Kingston here... Yes, yes. He's here with me. Mannon has reported back to his office. You should find him there." He ends the call.

Kingston says, "Professor, we're summoned to the Situation Room. Mannon was expecting trouble because the FBI led our, uh, delegation to the Senate hearing. I suspect we are about to find out how many bullets we've dodged by having him take the lead on that."

Chapter 32

Situation Room

Lots of brass is seated, including chair of joint chiefs Admiral Dunbar, Vice-President Pounds and a token woman wearing a lot of ribbons.

Kingston and Kurt walk in, followed shortly by Mannon.

Kingston grabs the initiative. "Gentlemen, lady. I am ready to brief you fully on recent events."

Pounds is not having it. "We are not here for a briefing. Your off-books operation has gone quite far enough. I am not sure why only one FBI agent is facing charges for killing a Supreme Court nominee but I have made it clear to your superiors that we cannot have more of this."

Kingston objects, trying to assert himself. "With respect, sir, you are not in charge..."

Dunbar asserts himself. "Well, I am. And I have conferred with Director Wraith and he wants Agent Mannon off the case too, pending Internal Affairs investigation of

100

whether he should also be charged."

Kingston says, "But the aliens..."

Pounds smirks. "Their ambassador filed a formal protest at your violation of their spacecraft but has been graceful enough to leave it at that."

Kingston tries to get the conversation back under control "We have evidence..."

Dunbar backs Pounds. "This is not a discussion. You will not interfere with any investigation related to the president, the shooting of the Supreme Court candidate or any matter related to the aliens. Dismissed."

Chapter 33

White House out

Mannon, Kingston and Kurt are led to their cars and escorted out via a side gate in convey.

As soon as they are well clear of the White House, they stop to confer. Kingston is livid. "Those damn fools! They are going to let the president get away with it. Agent, you may have a bit of work to do to clear this but you didn't do anything wrong."

Kurt says, "I am one person they have no jurisdiction over. A tenured professor has no boss. If only I had the DNA samples..."

"Since I am no longer on the case, maybe I won't need this." Mannon produces an evidence bag containing a water glass. "President's. Carefully cleaned of any other DNA before he touched it."

"Brilliant! I will take this over to the lab. I don't suppose you also have a sample from the Canadian?"

"That was the plan but I have no access to him or any other samples now."

"Damn. That could have added a useful piece to the puzzle. Agent, general, a pleasure working with you. I hope I still have something to contribute. General: stay in touch and I will do the best I can with what I can assemble in the lab."

"And your student."

"Absolutely, General. It was a stroke of good fortune that you accidentally read him in."

Chapter 34

FBI office

Harper is alone in an FBI office. The door opens; Captain Rivera walks in.

"Rivera! What are you doing here?"

"They asked me for a translator. I told them I can't do the job but I can find someone. But first I insisted on seeing you. Are you OK?"

"Nice of you to ask. You didn't seem the caring type."

"Whatever history we have, you know a lot about our operations."

"Well, I am not talking about that and they aren't asking. Kind of learned that from watching your TV act. You never know anything, right? All you have that I don't have is a fake military rank."

"OK, good. Nice to know you get it. I will send them one of our colleagues who follows the pings nearly as well as you. What are the feds doing with you?"

"Leaving me alone, mostly. As long as the president is resisting investigation, there is not much they can do."

"Well good luck. I brought you an old friend to show no hard feelings, eh?"

The door opens. An alien walks in: Antonio.

Harper jumps out of his chair in excitement. "Ant... !"

The alien holds a finger to what passes for its lips, a strangely human gesture. It passes a piece of paper to Harper who reads it then hands it back.

Antonio nods, again, looking very human in the way he moves despite the very non-human face and breaks out in the alien language. "PING PING PING PING PING PING PING PING PING PING PING PING."

Harper grins and nods energetically. "I get it."

Antonio follows up. "PING PING PING PING PING PING!"

"You bet!" Harper shakes Antonio's hand as the alien turns to leave.

Rivera waits for the door to close. "OK, I will make sure our embassy sends you a real lawyer. My guess is that once the aliens sort out between their factions, they will have no reason to keep you."

"Nice to hear you know a bit more than you admit on TV."

"My pay grade. Never forget your pay grade."

It's a strange, strange world we live in, Master Jack
No hard feelin's if I never come back
You're a very strange man and I thank you, Master Jack

Chapter 35

Coffee shop

Jane is sitting in a coffee shop and Kurt strides in. She gets up.

"So fantastic you could make it. So much going on. You must be working night and day in the lab."

"I am not sure how much more I can do. We are officially off the case. Though we can do some unofficial digging."

"What? ..."

"Better you don't know."

"So much I don't know. When Jack went to your office, I was sure you would be seriously hurt. I'm so ashamed that I was too cowardly to warn you."

"He tried to deliver a lesson in humility. He forgot which person in the room was the teacher."

"I am still surprised. You used to be..."

"... a lot softer. But that was before I enlisted. I never told you what unit I was in. Still can't. Let's just say I learned to look after myself."

"I wish I could bank the expression on his face when I asked how it went... If we get through all this..."

"We will. Don't you worry. Right now, I don't have a whole lot of head space to help you deal with Jack."

"Not a problem. I got a good divorce lawyer. Told him to shoot for a settlement. He isn't the kind who will end up with all the money, me with nothing."

"My old friend, still as practical as ever. You have great skills, you can move on from this, do well for yourself. Me, I signed up for the military in the toughest unit that would take me. Then, when I had enough of that, I signed up for another PhD. No one could call me practical." Kurt grins foolishly.

"Just a friend?"

"Give it time."

"For me to get over it?"

"No. I need time. And what is going on right now is a big distraction so don't tell me I have had enough time."

"Let's get coffee then. I like this place because it's full service. Makes it feel a bit less like supermarket coffee. I'll hail a waiter."

Chapter 36

University lab

Jamie and Karen are in the lab, Jamie studiously working through samples; Karen is watching news on a computer screen.

Kurt walks in and takes in the scene with a quick glance. "Pleased to see you made it here."

"In the chaos after the shooting no one thought to worry about the protesters outside. I just blended in. Like I belonged."

Karen nods. "Which you do."

Kurt produces the evidence bag. "Look what I brought you to work on. Fresh uncontaminated presidential DNA.

"Pity though we lost Harper. I would like to compare the two forms of cross-contaminated DNA."

Jamie points to his workbench. "What do you think I was grabbing before we left the mothership? I hoped we wouldn't lose him on the way out since we needed him to fly the dropship but it was easy enough to pocket his sample."

"And I thought you were frozen with fear."

"That too. You did tell me it's OK to be scared."

"Yet you kept your head and took something that could make a difference. Well done, soldier."

Karen rounds on Kurt. "Just so you know, I am not happy that you are turning my boy into a soldier. This guy will not even step on an ant."

"I meant it in a totally respectful way. Just as your protest was fighting a battle even if it is not by lethal means. Jamie, where are we with processing DNA samples?"

"I am starting to do reads of the president's DNA. That I can do but you are the master coder, prof. I will need a lot of help on analysis."

Karen isn't ready to change the subject. "That shooting was pretty scary. Excuse me if I do not get the soldier thing. While I did not want that creepy con artist on the Supreme Court, that was pretty extreme."

Kurt nods grimly. "Have you seen the footage? He brandished an alien weapon and shouted 'Stupid humans! I'll kill you all!' The agent who shot him didn't know the weapon couldn't fire."

"I didn't see that. Maybe I should check it out and leave you two to do the lab stuff."

Kurt turns to Jamie. "What's this about not stepping on an ant? Biology is not for the squeamish."

"I focus my electives on lab work with samples like DNA, nothing that involves cruelty to small animals. Think of this from the ant's perspective. To them we are ambulatory food mountains."

"We are what?"

"Every part of a human, to an ant, is edible and delicious. On a vast, incomprehensible scale. Put yourself there. You are starved. You spot a massive mountain of pizza, bigger than the eye can see. You rush up to take a nibble and plan on taking some home to the starving family. Suddenly, a portion of it, still too big to comprehend, lifts up and stomps on you.

"I don't stomp on ants."

"You're a weird kid."

Jamie switches focus. "On the plus side, the aliens don't have a majority on the Supreme Court. What happens though, if there's a tied vote? Does the Chief Justice have a casting vote?"

Karen, finally on her way out, turns back. "No. They can't overturn a lower court on a tied vote. So even if the Chief Justice was one of them, which she's not, it wouldn't help them. But alien majority or not, they *do* have a conservative majority."

Karen leaves.

Jamie says, "I just thought of something. We have a microscope where we can see chromosomes."

"So?"

"Genetics 101. Humans have 23 pairs of chromosomes. That would be a dead simple thing to count compared with detailed DNA analysis. Or even isolating the virus and working out a PCR test."

"Not that simple."

"Yeah, but I told you I'm good in the lab. We have 4 variations. Straight human, which we know already. Human contaminated with alien from the Canadian, alien contaminated with human from our president and pure alien off the weapon."

"OK, so get to it. I forgot about the blood on the weapon. Where did you. . . ?"

"Took a swab on the way down. . ."

"Good lad. I am going to talk to Kingston and Mannon to see if we can make any official input even if they're off the case."

Chapter 37

Oval Office

Jack is in the Oval Office with some generic aides. He has a new translator, Juan Ramos, neatly dressed in an inexpensive suit, sporting a USCS badge.

The aides are proffering papers across the Resolute and Jack is shuffling them impatiently without paying much attention to the contents, signing where directed.

Corleone walks in. "Mr President. A private word."

Jack: "PING PING PING PING PING!"

Ramos yells, sweeping his arm around the room then pointing at the door, "Everyone out! Scram!"

All but the translator, Jack and Corleone leave.

Corleone says, "Mr President, I like the way he talks. But I am afraid the translator has to go too. Very confidential."

"PING PING PING!"

Ramos leaves, crestfallen.

"It is a matter of time before the Democrats move to impeach. My sources say they are looking for a pretext."

"PING PING PING?"

"The Speaker is opposed to it and is worried that it may harden your support as it did with the Clinton impeachment but we must be prepared."

"PING PING."

"I take that as a yes."

Jack nods.

"Tactics for the impeachment. We are on new ground here so best thing is if we never get to the evidence."

"PING PING PING?"

"I am taking that as a question. What I mean is everyone the House subpoenas, we say is an executive privilege and security issue."

Jack nods vigorously. "PING PING – PING!"

"Quite. We can tie everything up in court until well after the election when the whole thing will be moot."

"PING PING PING PING PING PING PING PING... PING!"

"Which I take as meaning you intend to use every trick in the book and win big."

Jack nods even more vigorously.

"Mr President, we understand each other perfectly. Who needs a translator?"

Chapter 38

Coffee shop

Kurt is back in his newly favourite coffee shop, sitting with Mannon, waiting for Kingston.

Kingston arrives. "Sit, gentlemen. This is all informal."

"No disrespect, but I wasn't about to stand and salute. Professor now..."

"Yeah. No doubt also why you are still on the case and we are off."

"Not officially of course. But they can't stop me working in my own lab. Not without a warrant and I have not given cause for that yet."

"And you are about to change that?" Mannon asks.

"Well, my lab happens to have three samples to compare with human DNA. Alien, alien we believe to be contaminated with human and human we believe to be contaminated with alien."

Mannon grins slyly. "And somehow you've acquired a

sample of another alien contaminated by human." He pushes an evidence bag towards Kurt. Kingston's eyebrows rise.

A waiter shows up and they pause as she takes orders.

Kurt says, "Ah. And that would be. . . ?"

"A certain shooting that got me off the case."

Kingston shakes his head. "This is even more off-books than what we were doing before. Where does this take us?"

Kurt says, "General, do you not have any contacts who could use any information we unearth? Unofficially, behind the scenes, stir things up?"

"Sure. But there are limits to what we can actually do. It's not like this is the badlands of Afghanistan."

"I am not so sure. And I spent a long time there."

Three cups arrive: cappuccino for Mannon, espresso for Kurt, long black for Kingston. The waiter leaves.

Kingston sips his. "How much time do you need for the lab work?"

"Depends on Jamie. Says he's good. May have results by the time I get back; maybe tomorrow. I hope I don't need to get more help."

Kurt's phone chirps. "Excuse me. . . " He listens and nods a few times and thanks the caller.

"OK, the kid's better than I thought, even if I had to write all his code. We have a result. Alien DNA has 25 chromosomes. Human, even contaminated with alien, still 23. Alien contaminated with human, 27."

"So we could use this to. . . ?" Mannon asks

Kurt says, "If this checks out with any more samples so we can be sure, we could work up a quick test for alien.

Ideally one that doesn't need us toting around a lab and a thousand-X microscope. Once we analyze the alien virus and how it alters DNA, there are other test strategies we could use, but this is much quicker."

Kingston finishes his long black. "I will keep my ear to the ground for now – discrete, not say anything."

Mannon nods, his cappuccino untouched.

"I will let you know if we find out more. If you guys can find out who is safe to talk to for now, that would be a start. Best I get back to the lab." Kurt knocks back his espresso as they all stand up.

"I'll get this," says Mannon, summoning the waiter to pay.

Chapter 39

Jack rally

Jack is at a podium – ho hum – amidst the now-boring sea of bright orange PAFA-hats.

"PING PING PING PING! … PING!"

"PAFA! PAFA! PAFA!"

Jack holds up poster: DEEP STATE PLOT! DON'T BE-LIEVE A THING!

Then another: FAKE NEWS!

The crowd goes crazy.

Furious yells break out and blur into a chant. "LOCK THEM UP! LOCK THEM UP!"

Jack closes with the obvious. "PING PING PING PING!"

Zoom out to the ever-present enclosing Twitter stream

The True Lib @deepStateBlue: Clearly alien. Hang on every word even though you actually don't know what he's saying. Mind you, you did that before

118

when he contradicted himself and told obvious lies.

Jack fan @Jackfan: We understand just fine! #PAFA! Witch hunt!

The True Lib @deepStateBlue: Rude to call an alien a witch.

Jack fan @Jackfan: #PAFA! Best president ever! #Jack third term!

The True Lib @deepStateBlue: He has to make it through the first one. #ImpeachJack

---

Jack fan @Jackfan: #DeepState plot! Murdered Kernighan!

The True Lib @deepStateBlue: Aren't all Jack supporters for 2nd amendment and open carry?

Chapter 40

Coffee shop reprised

Jane and Kurt are already sitting in the usual coffee shop and their waiter is walking away after taking their order.

"Great to see you again, Jane. How's the divorce going?"

"It's going. His guy's talking to my guy and they should have some numbers soon."

"Still not planning to fight?"

"What's the point? The president's an alien and no one is doing a damn thing about it."

"It's a strange, strange world we live in, Master Jack."

"Still with that song? Jack isn't a master of anything any more."

"Yeah, weird, I can't get it out of my head. Not just your Jack; the president fits the lyrics somehow too. We don't want him to be 'master' in any sense either."

"But what can we do?"

"Plenty of protests..."

"There's always protests."

"Could be more than that. Nothing that I can talk about though. Nothing official, just stuff I am doing on the side in my lab."

"My old softie. Now the whole world depends on you." She puts a hand on his.

"Does it? So much craziness, so many people who could put a stop to it. Yet nothing is done. Why did we bother passing the 25th if we can't use it now?"

Their coffees arrive and they discuss lunch options with the waiter.

Chapter 41

Canadian alien camp

At the dry, dusty plain just inside the Canadian border, the mothership is back overhead. We see the same scene as before but with a smaller convoy this time, distinctly less armoured: Toyota pickups.

The convoy stops at an alien-run checkpoint built out of shacks, slightly in from the USCS-controlled main gate.

Captain Rivera exits the lead vehicle. He bashes on a random panel of the checkpoint – no part of it is clearly a door. "Hello! The Americans have promised us aid. Can you send out a leader to talk?"

An alien emerges. Evidently part of the checkpoint shack is in fact a door. "PING PING PING PING PING PING."

Rivera holds up a hand. "Not so fast! I am not used to your accent!

"We need to know what will make the biggest difference here."

"PING PING PING PING PING PING."

"Yeah, we can replace some of the shacks. We can bring containers..."

"PING PING PING PING PING PING PING PING PING PING PING."

"The Americans are only giving us three hundred million dollars, we can't build houses for that."

"PING PING PING PING PING PING."

"And anyway, your people are all supposed to go home some time soon, not so?"

"PING PING PING PING PING PING."

"Yeah, I want to know where the American money is too. They promised, then nothing."

The alien slams the door in his face and the shack shakes precariously. It is no longer clear which part of it is a door.

A dropship swoops down from the mothership menacingly. Rivera jumps into the lead vehicle, seconds ahead of the rest of his crew, and beats a hasty retreat.

Chapter 42

Breaking World News: BWN

We are back to the anchor duet.

"Jake, the Republicans have just announced that they're cancelling primaries in three more states. Do they not understand that their candidate is most likely an alien and could be disqualified at any moment?"

"I have given up making sense of the Republican strategy. You are either a never-Jacker or an ever-Jacker."

"Meanwhile the Democratic field keeps growing. Every time President Jack expands the limits of acceptable presidential behaviour, they expand their number of candidates. Isn't this adding confusion to their message?"

"You would think so. The more it appears that anyone could beat the Jack re-election campaign, they seem to miss the point that there is a difference between 'anyone' and 'everyone'."

"Hold up, Jake. Breaking news. The president is calling for Second Amendment supporters to show up in numbers at rallies across the country. What is that all about?"

"Not just show up, but show up armed. This seems to be a new variant on his call to storm the White House."

"The one that fizzled, when about twenty people showed up?"

"Let's go to the White House."

Chapter 43

White House briefing room

Presidential spokesperson Stephanie Spicer strides out aside Jack, now looking fully alien.

"The president has asked me to speak for him until he can get this speech thing sorted out."

Jack nods. "PING PING PING PING PING PING!"

"He has called mass rallies across the country to show opposition to repealing the Second Amendment. He cannot be there in person at each but will appear on a massive screen so he can be with his people."

"PING PING PING PING PING PING PING PING PING PING."

Garcia interrupts. "Mr President, who exactly is threatening to repeal the Second?"

Jack says, "PING PING PING PING PING PING?"

"Who isn't?" Spicer replies for him. "The Republicans of course. In practical terms, the Democrats are attempting to do so by banning what they call assault weapons and to introduce unconstitutional background checks. This president will never stand for that."

Garcia adds, "But that is not the same thing as repealing; even if they pass the law, which hasn't happened yet, it can be tested in the courts."

"PING PING PING PING PING PING PING PING PING PING. PING PING PING PING PING PING PING PING PING PING!"

Spicer angrily responds, "I didn't offer you a follow-up. But the president would like to point out that his last Supreme Court nominee was assassinated."

Chapter 44

PAFA rally

A Jack surrogate is now at the podium, a bit incongruous against the sea of bright orange PAFA-hats; Jack is on multiple big screens surrounding the crowd, visible from all angles.

Jack Surrogate roars: "Put America First Again! Yeah!"

"PAFA! PAFA! PAFA!"

"Show us your weapons!"

"PAFA! PAFA! PAFA!" Rifles and handguns are waved in great profusion.

"Open carry everywhere! It is your Constitutional Right! Twenty rallies around the country, a million people all defending the Second Amendment!"

"PAFA! PAFA! PAFA!" Weapons are waved with gusto.

"So many good guys with guns! That is what keeps this country safe!"

"PAFA! PAFA! PAFA!" More weapons are lofted.

"GOOD GUYS WITH GUNS!" Raucous cheers follow; there is an air of self-congratulation.

"GOOD GUYS WITH GUNS!" The goodness is clearly bountiful beyond measure.

Chapter 45

Breaking World News: BWN

We are back at the BWN two-anchor show.

"Jake, opinions vary on whether it is actually a million people. But a lot of people have rallied with a lot of guns."

'Yes. A tinder box. Let us hope sense prevails and it is all just for show."

"Of course the stats say that we have the highest level of gun violence in the world but I am not going to argue with a good guy with a gun."

'They did not go through with their threat to hold rallies in states where open carry is illegal."

"Well, Jake, they are threatening to run the next round countrywide, which will be interesting. Including states that are not open carry. How do you arrest a stadium full of people with AR-15s?"

"How, indeed?"

"Then there's the question of why the president was not there in person."

"Could he be afraid that a good guy with a gun would accidentally shoot in his direction?"

"An absurd thought. Good guys with guns. What could go wrong?"

The tweets at this point are way too predictable so we skip them.

Chapter 46

Jamie and Karen's apartment

We zoom out from a TV showing the rally and BWN studio to find Jamie and Karen at home for once. It is a typical student apartment – not much more space than is needed for cooking and sleeping with a minimal bathroom. It is, however, atypically-student-tidy.

Jamie turns from the TV. "Explain this to me. Second Amendment fundamentalists say it is there to stop the state from being more powerful than the people. Yet most of them back authoritarian politicians like Jack."

"I am only a straight-A law student. What do I know?"

"Has there ever been a case where armed citizens have forced the government to be less authoritarian?"

"Only example I can think of is when the Black Panthers urged black people to arm themselves against police brutality. That may have had some effect. For a while. The NRA back then decided that gun regulation was a good thing. That was then. This is now. So the logic is different."

"Me, I will stick with easy stuff like DNA analysis, where the principles stay the same. Join me at the lab again tomorrow?"

"Sure. Though I can only offer moral support."

Chapter 47

Breaking World News: BWN

In the BWN newsroom, an anchor intones dramatically, "In breaking news, a whistleblower allegation has surfaced. An anonymous intelligence official has claimed that the president made some disturbing statements on a call to the alien ambassador."

The front page of a statement scrolls past:

```
UNCLASSIFIED

July 31 Presidential
phone call

Early in the morning
of July 31, the President
spoke by telephone with
```

```
the alien ambassador
to the United States.

The president sought
to involve the aliens
in investigating Democratic
complicity in the change
in his body to alien
form and in the shooting
of Judge Kernighan.

He also specifically
authorised the aliens
to deal with Rudi Corleone.

White House officials
told me they were extremely
concerned at this call
because the president
was using his office
for personal gain.
```

"I have with me Dana Ansell, BWN chief White House correspondent. Dana, what is the significance of this disclosure?"

"Jake, if this stands up, it is very significant. The president may not use his office for personal favours. If there were a legitimate suspicion of criminal action he should have handed it over to the Department of Justice. Done like this, he appears to be involving an outside power in his re-election campaign."

"Is this impeachable conduct?"

"That very much depends on the Democrats. And what else may be unearthed."

"I am still reading through the complaint. There's more: he promises the aliens he will pay over funds he has been withholding for upgrading the alien site if they announce an investigation."

"Wow. Just wow. I am speechless."

"Dana, that must be a first for you. Obviously this will have to be investigated but on first sight he has been using foreign aid as a lever to dig up dirt on his political opponents. How can that not be impeachable?"

"Indeed. What remains to be seen is what solid evidence will appear that backs up the whistleblower."

We take a break from rationality to view tweets once again. Zoom out to Twitter.

Jack fan @Jackfan: #DeepState plot! Best president ever! Entitled to investigate corrupt libtards!

The True Lib @deepStateBlue: And using aliens to do his dirty work?

Jack fan @Jackfan: You believe the lying fake news? #Deepstate plot! Coupe!

The True Lib @deepStateBlue: I think
you mean coup. But then again, I don't
know if you know what you mean.

Jack fan @Jackfan: #PAFA!

The True Lib @deepStateBlue: What does
#PAFA stand for? Put Aliens First
Always?

Chapter 48

Canadian alien camp

The mothership drifts serenely overhead. Nothing below is serene. Dropships are buzzing angrily, there are ground fighting machines in profusion and blue flashes in all directions.

Human guards are scattering beyond the perimeter and some of the aliens are running chaotically from the camp, with no hint of organization.

We zoom out to the BWN studio with the Canadian alien camp scene in backdrop. Our two anchors are together in the studio.

"Jake, it seems like all-out factional war between aliens. Any comment from the White House? What is happening with the held-back aid?"

"I have just been talking to our White House correspondent, Dana Ansell. I am trying to get a hook up to her. Seems the Alien Ambassador is in the winning faction. Let's see if we can connect now."

Ansell appears on screen. "I have just left a White House briefing. The Alien Ambassador was there and through an interpreter assured us that the rebel faction was being brought under control as we speak."

"Dana, where did they find an interpreter? The aliens can't pronounce our languages."

"Judging from the accent, I would say a Canadian. However the interpreter wasn't introduced and was kept out of sight."

Anchor Jake chimes in. "Dana, it certainly looks from the footage on screen as if those in control of the mothership also have the most powerful weapons. But how do we know which faction is which? And do we know if the president is part of all this?"

"Excellent questions. We can only go on what we are told and who knows how much of that is true, with President Jack's track record?"

Chapter 49

University lab

We are back in Kurt's lab; the TV is in the background, show-ing the BWN studio as the discussion with Dana Ansell tails off. Jamie and Karen are with Kurt; all are watching.

Kurt breaks the silence. "Crazy! We don't even know if the aliens talking to the president are his own faction, or Cy's."

"Or the Canadian's missing friends. The other faction," adds Jamie.

Karen points out, "Remember, Cy isn't a faction."

"Ambulatory food mountain."

"What, that again?" Kurt shakes his head. "We aren't working on ants here."

"I am thinking us versus the aliens."

Karen looks puzzled. "You mean they see us as food?"

"No, just the general difference in perception. They are super-advanced compared with us. They can do interstellar travel using physics totally beyond us and have unimaginably powerful weapons. Right now, they are a bit down on their luck and we treat them worse than the most despised human refugees."

"Which is not right even for our own..."

"Yes, and we have an apparently xenophobic president who insists on building a wall along the entire Canadian border as if this is a permanent, unsolvable problem when he knows better himself."

Kurt takes the focus back to the lab. "Yeah, right. Let's focus on a problem we can actually solve. How are those results looking, Jamie?"

"Good. I have a straightforward test now that can tell apart human, alien and alien converted to human. It would be a bit more work to screen for a case like the Canadian, human contaminated with alien."

Kurt nods. "But that's not a big problem right now. We don't even know where Harper is. None of my government contacts will talk to me about that. I may have the highest clearance but..."

"... need to know." Jamie completes.

"Exactly. But what we do have is a reliable test to root out any more cases like Jack. And his judges. But: what to do with it? Karen, you know a bit about the law, not so?"

"With probable cause you could get a search warrant or even a grand jury. But that doesn't help with the president. As long as DoJ sticks to its policy of not indicting a sitting president, none of that sort of process is much good."

"And the fake human judges?"

"In principle, we could go after them, but we would have to have a plausible explanation of how we obtained a sample even if it was just to get a search warrant."

"And someone in government to act on it. Mannon is *persona non grata* and I don't know anyone else in the FBI."

Jamie asks, "And his contacts?"

"Worth a try. Let me call him."

Kurt tries the phone. "Damn! Not picking up. I don't want to leave a message; that can't help if he's in trouble. Kingston is even more out of the picture. So no point trying him."

"Not risky even calling him?"

"Maybe, Jamie. Maybe. But we need some official contact. Let me talk to some of my vet buddies. I know where to find some. Favourite bar. Some have connections in law enforcement."

"A bar? At this time of day?"

"Kid, did no one tell you *anything* about PTSD?"

Chapter 50

Breaking World News: BWN

The first Democratic primary debate is about to start. Twenty candidates are on stage. BWN does the usual dual-anchor show.

"The first Democratic debate is about to kick off. With twenty candidates. President Jack is so far underwater in the polls that virtually anyone could beat him."

"Possibly. But as we keep pointing out, even if *anyone* could *everyone* can't because too many candidates on stage at once drown each other out."

"Unless one of them is super-bizarre or weird."

"You mean like Jack."

"You said it, not me."

Chapter 51

Bar

Kurt and Damian are talking earnestly. Kurt's beer is untouched; Damian's is rather more touched. They obviously know each other well and exchange typical comrades-in-arms banter. Of the two Kurt is clearly the one who's kept in shape. Damian is slouched over his beer, a bit of a gut developing, sad eyes that don't take in much.

Kurt takes the conversation to the main point. "You used to know people in the law."

"Yeah, because they bailed me out. Understood that some vets struggle to adapt to society. I owe them big time, not the other way around."

"Thing is, I am not looking for a favour, just a way to get the attention of someone who can..."

"... bend the law a bit for you. I call that a favour."

"It is not a favour if it isn't for my personal benefit."

"I'm listening. Skeptical but listening."

"My lab has samples of alien DNA and the president's DNA that show he's an alien. And we now have reliable, simple tests to find other aliens fast."

"Man, whatever you're smoking, I want some."

"Damian! This is serious. Our president is an alien. And to make it worse, the aliens have split into factions and we have no idea who is on which side."

"Who is on which side? Humans or aliens?"

Kurt's head lands in his hands. "Damn! We actually know nothing. I am just reasonably sure that anyone who has been in government longer than Jack has been around is probably safe. Come on, who do you know?"

"OK, I have some ideas. Who do you want? A straight shooter? Or a risk taker who could get herself fired?"

"First kind – but keep the other in reserve. Give me some names. And a bit of background so I know how they work."

Chapter 52

Breaking World News: BWN

At the House press briefing, Speaker Mike McNamara and House Judiciary Committee Chair Jane Gingrich are about to speak. In the BWN studio, the usual dual-anchor commentary opens.

"In breaking news, we have heard that the Democrats are about to announce an impeachment hearing. Let's go to it live now."

The studio disappears, leaving the focus on Speaker McNamara. "It is my sad duty to announce that the House has no option but to launch an impeachment enquiry. In addition to the whistleblower report, we have a number of other witnesses willing to testify to unlawful conduct by the president. This includes conspiracy to involve a foreign power in his election campaign, corrupting his office to meet private ends and broadly acting corruptly."

Gingrich takes her turn. "The House Judiciary Committee will shortly be announcing the rules for the enquiry."

"This is not the route we wished to take but the president's conduct has left us no option. The whistleblower report was concerning enough but his attempts at shutting down our enquiry on the substance added the potential charge of obstruction. It's a sad day for America." McNamara looks suitably grim and hands back to Gingrich.

Gingrich is uncharacteristically playing the Good Cop. "Members of my committee have considerable experience as prosecutors and have studied the Nixon and Clinton impeachments. We will attempt to obtain cooperation from the administration. If there is nothing to hide we can deal with this expeditiously. We hope the president and his aides will respond to subpoenas and requests for evidence in a constructive spirit of getting this over and done with with minimum disruption as we head towards the election."

We zoom back to the studio and the opening anchor resumes.

"Jake, what are the odds of that?"

"When we have a breaking news story of hell freezing over. Right after that."

Chapter 53

Canadian alien camp

We are back at the Canadian camp.

The mothership floats lazily overhead, still at odds with the scene below though less so than before. Dropships are buzzing busily and there are ground fighting machines in profusion but no blue flashes. All is calm.

There are human guards far outside the perimeter, watching heavily armed aliens return to the camp, herding others, obviously defeated.

Nothing to see here. Move on.

Chapter 54

University lab

The TV in the background of Kurt's lab is showing BWN, alternating between the Democratic debate and the Canadian alien camp. Jamie and Karen are watching the screen when Kurt walks in.

"You kids been watching TV all day?"

"Well, not all day. But Jamie ran out of things to do. What took you so long?"

"Long story short; I got us another FBI contact. Well connected, may be able to open some doors. After trying half a dozen others who either would not take my call or dropped me as soon as they heard who I was.

"Jamie, how's your report on the testing method coming along?"

"Done. Emailed to you." Jamie holds up small stack of paper. "Hard copy if you need it."

"And test kit?"

"Ready to rock and roll." Jamie holds up a small plastic box. "Enough here to do a dozen tests, easy to make more."

"OK, let's go then. FBI dude has a car outside. Karen, it's already a problem that Jamie is not cleared."

"I guess not much I can do to help anyway. I will be at home. Call me if you need me."

Chapter 55

House impeachment hearing

Judiciary Committee Chair Jane Gingrich gavels to order. Present: various Representatives and Jack's lawyer, Corleone.

Gingrich addresses Corleone. "Having heard the case by the House prosecutor, we now turn to the defense. You have 45 minutes for your opening remarks. Counsel?"

Corleone stares down his mike. "The House has presented a long list of witnesses it intends to call. All of those witnesses work closely with the president so there will be issues of executive privilege and national security. We intend to oppose any subpoenas that endanger the national interest."

Zoom out to BWN studio. The usual anchors have a guest. "We turn now to constitutional law expert Bradly Simms of Stanford Law School. Professor, do you see any indication in what the president's counsel said of where they are going with this?"

"What he is doing is laying the basis for protracted court battles to ensure that nothing happens before the election."

"And then what?"

"If he loses, nothing, as you can't impeach someone who's not in office. If he doesn't, it all depends how strong the Republicans are in the House and Senate."

The other anchor takes a turn. "What options are open to the Democrats?"

"It very much depends on what witnesses they can garner. At the very least they may try pushing obstruction as the main charge. This is perfectly valid legally but, remember, impeachment is more political than legal. How this pans out very much depends on public opinion.

"Even if the House impeaches, they still need to get a conviction in the Senate and the Democrats don't have the numbers to do that. So really you do not want a legal scholar here. You want a political pundit because this is very much an issue of how this plays out to the election."

Chapter 56

Outside White House

Pro and anti Jack protesters jostle for attention and position with competing posters of the like of

DEEP STATE: PAFA

NO DICTATOR

NO KING JACK

JACK THIRD TERM

The White House is in the distance. The usual late afternoon DC traffic is uninterrupted.

From one side there are loud chants of "PAFA! PAFA! Jack third term! Deep state conspiracy!"

The competing chants are "Impeach! Impeach! Lock *him*

up!"

Both sides make a compelling case. To themselves.

The traffic continues to flow by without incident no matter how loud the chants. The White House looks just the same.

Chapter 57

Durham's SUV

Durham's Hollywood-standard black SUV is parked in a quiet side street. Kurt gets into the front seat, Jamie the back.

"Agent Durham. Jamie is one of my students, inadvertently read in by General Kingston, now our top expert on testing for alien DNA."

"I won't ask. But to get anywhere with this we need probable cause, search warrants and the like."

'You can do that?"

"It's my job. But we may need a little creativity. How much time does your test take, Jamie?"

"If we have a good DNA sample, we can do it in about a minute. To confirm to a skeptic, we would need to isolate the cellular DNA and use a 1000X microscope, maybe 30 minutes – standard lab technique."

"To reveal what?"

"Alien and human DNA have a different number of chromosomes, alien converted to human different again. Standard lab technique, any competent microbiologist can do it. It's only needed if someone doesn't trust my test."

Kurt asks, "Say we get past that point. What next?"

"If the president is the suspect, there is little we can do. It's Congress's job to police the president. The House can impeach based on whatever evidence they see fit but then it's over to the Senate and if the president has a majority in the Senate, they will need very strong evidence to convict. Particularly with the opposition in disarray. Purely an opinion based on observation. Not taking a partisan position, you understand."

Kurt nods. "Absolutely. My old buddy told me you're a pro. The House has already started to impeach so we need to tread carefully."

Durham starts the car. "Let's go. I have other agents I can work with, who can push this thing along."

Chapter 58

Canadian alien camp

The mothership is overhead, barely moving. A single drop-ship is lazily patrolling; all is calm on the ground.

Zoom out: human guards in USCS livery have been replaced by aliens at the main gate.

Nothing to see here. Really.

Chapter 59

FBI office

Durham ushers Kurt and Jamie into his office then faces them across his desk.

"OK so aside from the president, who else do you suspect of being an alien in disguise?"

Kurt says, "Supreme court justices Jack appointed."

"Which of them?"

"*All* of them. Including the one that one of your agents shot."

"Wow."

"I've heard that the DoJ has a policy not to indict a sitting president. Does that apply to a supreme court judge?" Jamie asks.

"Probably not. The presidential policy relates to separation of powers though it hasn't been tested in the courts. As far as I know, no sitting Supreme Court Justice has been indicted. But I can see no obstacle – except we need to work out what the crime is."

"If they are aliens, they aren't US citizens. Wouldn't that make their position illegal?" Asks Kurt.

"This may be something of a surprise, but the Constitution does not require US citizenship for appointment as a Supreme Court justice."

Jamie looks shocked. "What? Does this mean we can do nothing?"

"Not entirely. Appropriations law prohibits federal employees who are not citizens, green card holders or refugees from being paid a federal salary."

Kurt looks unconvinced. "That doesn't sound very strong. If they really are aliens it will not worry them too much if they have to work without pay."

"Beyond that, Kurt, Congress has the the power to impeach and remove a Supreme Court justice, much the same way as a president. Which is already happening for Jack. So why not go to the House?"

Kurt signals that he has not quite given up on law enforcement. "In practical terms, what you have that no one can contest is the body of Kernighan. You can get someone else to check the DNA the way we did. All they need is to isolate cellular DNA and count the chromosomes. If they dig deeper they will find more discrepancies."

Jamie adds, "And the Canadian. . . "

"Right, I forgot him. Agent, do you have access to him?"

Durham says, "What would you expect to find if you can run your tests, Jamie?"

"A standard human has 23 pairs of chromosomes, an alien

25, an alien contaminated with human, 27. A human contaminated with alien still has 23."

"So the Canadian doesn't add much? Do I understand correctly, Kurt?"

"We didn't have time to check him out in detail. We have a sample that we've partially sequenced that has some oddities, though nothing we found affects function. The fact that he can use alien tech means there must be a clear difference from human. Jamie, any ideas?"

"What about trying to isolate something in the anomalies in his DNA that lights up the alien weapons? A novel protein they encode, perhaps?"

"If we still had one of the weapons, we could work on that. Any chance...?"

"No, Kurt. I can't release evidence like that to you. What you have given me is a big help. I can source independent DNA experts but I will have to go through the official command chain."

Kurt stands up and thanks Durham, then adds: "I guess we may end up going to the House. But I am worried that they will see showing that the judges are aliens as a sideshow, with the president already facing impeachment."

Chapter 60

University lab

Back in the lab, the TV is in the background, showing the BWN studio. But no one is paying attention. Jamie, Karen and Kurt are deeply engrossed in discussing the way forward..

The Canadian alien camp scene is in backdrop, as the two anchors have at it.

"Jake, it seems like the factional war between the aliens is over."

"The White House is keeping very quiet but rumours are that the aid is finally being released."

"Let's go to White House correspondent Dana Ansell. Dana, any announcement from the president?"

"Nothing as yet but we hear from Office of Management and Budget insiders that the aid has indeed been released."

"We have been trying to get comment from the Canadian government and their security contractor, USCS. We have nothing as yet. We will update this breaking story as soon as we have new information."

All this is lost on the lab occupants as Kurt summarizes where they're at: "Well, we haven't managed to get anywhere yet. I will talk to Durham again to see if he's opened any doors."

"I am not holding my breath. I have a big protest to attend. Joining me, Jamie?" Karen heads for the door.

Jamie stands up. "I'm in. Kurt? Just this once?"

"Love to join you kids but I must chase up the FBI. And I'm seeing Jane tonight."

Karen grins. "Great, you need a bit of time out. This thing is getting pretty intense, no sign of letting up."

Chapter 61

Outside White House

There's a huge crowd outside the White House. Posters and banners display numerous messages. This is a representative sample:

NO FOREIGN INFLUENCE

NO TO STOLEN ELECTIONS

ALIENS GOOD, ILLEGAL ALIENS BAD

DEFEND ROE V. WADE

GUN SANITY NOW

NO KING JACK

Jamie and Karen are just two of many faces in a big angry crowd.

For once, the PAFA-hats are nowhere to be seen. The crowd, lacking a counter, slowly loses intensity and starts to drift away. We zoom out and there are people further than the eye can see.

Chapter 62

Breaking World News: BWN

The twin-anchor show takes up the description of the scene. "Jake, anti-Jack protests are growing as Jack rallies scale up."

"That protest this afternoon was one of the biggest yet. Let's go live to the rally in Dallas. Once again, there is a Jack surrogate."

"And of course there's the Jack presence on big screens, safe from good guys with guns."

*   *   *   *

The Jack surrogate is at the podium amidst a sea of bright orange PAFA-hats; Jack once again surrounds the crowd on big screens.

Jack Surrogate: "Put America First Again! Yeah!"

Crowd chants: "PAFA! PAFA! PAFA!"

Jack Surrogate: "Show us your weapons!"

Crowd: "PAFA! PAFA! PAFA!"

Jack Surrogate: "Open carry everywhere! It is your Constitutional Right! Rallies in every state, millions defending the Second Amendment!"

Crowd: "PAFA! PAFA! PAFA!" Weapons are waved all round the stadium with gusto.

Jack Surrogate: "Good guys with guns! Defend democracy against the Democrats!"

Crowd: "PAFA! PAFA! GOOD GUYS WITH GUNS! GOOD GUYS WITH GUNS!"

Jack's multiscreen presence does a passable imitation of a beam for a non-human face, showing unmistakable glee. The crowd goes apeshit.

*   *   *   *

We focus back on the BWN studio and the regular duo.

"Jake, this is far bigger than the first rallies. And for the first time, openly challenges laws against open carry."

"That failed attempt at storming the White House also challenged open carry."

"True. But not on this scale."

"Yes, this is something big. A president openly defying the law *at the same time as being impeached*. Who ever imagined that happening?"

"This is what they threatened during the first round of rallies. As I said back then, who is going to arrest a stadium full of people with AR-15s?"

"What a mess. Who would've believed the American people could so easily be duped?"

Zoom out of the video to tweets. They are as enlightening as ever.

Jack fan @Jackfan: #FakeNews! Libtards are the ones being duped!

The True Lib @deepStateBlue: Show us the alien that we believe to be human.

Jack fan @Jackfan: We will show the libtards! Open carry everywhere!

The True Lib @deepStateBlue: More like mayhem everywhere.

Jack fan @Jackfan: We are stopping a coupe!!

The True Lib @deepStateBlue: That's coup. Never mind. By Stopping you mean Starting.

Jack fan @Jackfan: #PAFA!

The True Lib @deepStateBlue: And you

also aren't a sheep, right?

Jack fan @Jackfan: Can a sheep use an AR-15?

The True Lib @deepStateBlue: Obviously a PAFA sheep can.

Chapter 63

Jane's apartment

Jane answers a knock on the door. Kurt enters, wine bottle in hand, and delivers a brief kiss on her cheek. Master Jack starts playing.

Kurt says, "Oh. You found that song."

"Seems it means a lot to you."

"Not really. Just that the words seem to fit our situation so well."

"Our situation?"

"Me. What happened to you. The state of the world."

"Not *us*?"

"Dunno, maybe. Getting there. I still don't get how you ended up with Jack."

"You seemed to be so focused on your pain over losing Melissa."

"To a jerk. Then you married a jerk."

"Then you disappeared to Afghanistan. My sensitive,

vulnerable Kurt. Now look at you. A genuine if unsung war hero, taking on the system in a way I would never have believed."

"Well, maybe that sensitive vulnerable kid is still in here somewhere. But protected by a lot of walls."

"Walls can also form a jail."

"Maybe. Or a phoney political slogan as with Jack. The other one, not yours. But you invited me for dinner. I haven't eaten all day – chasing the stupid FBI. Watching kids protesting outside the White House. Wondering why it is always up to the kids. You know, like with the climate crisis. Always left up to the kids."

Jane clenches her lips. "Including going to war."

"Including going to war. Should we attack my merlot?"

"Yes, that's a war I can relate to."

Chapter 64

Breaking World News: BWN

The second Democratic debate has started with opening statements and is about to switch to questions from the moderator. Fifteen candidates are on stage.

BWN anchors set the scene. "The second Democratic debate is underway. Despite President Jack's unprecedented negative rating, no one has clearly broken through."

"No real standout opening statement. Perhaps Mayor Flanders's team advised him to tone it down?"

We switch to the debate and the moderator is taking charge. "We will take the first round of questions in turn from my left. Each candidate has 30 seconds and I will ask a follow up.

"Senator O'Keefe. What is your view of the recent open carry rallies?"

"Crazy, just crazy. We have the worst gun violence problem in the world and we should be bringing this under control not making it worse. If open carry is illegal, it is not political leadership to defy the law like this. Totally in line with the Jack presidency's disdain for the law and constitution."

The moderator adds, "Senator, they are arguing that open carry is consistent with the constitution and laws against open carry..."

"That is not what this country is about! If they really believe that they can go to the courts."

Flanders interjects. "That is so weak! We should be calling out the National Guard to put a stop to this!"

"Excuse me, Mayor Flanders," the moderate says briskly, "please wait your turn."

Flanders will not be shut down. "This is not the time to be polite or to wait your turn! We have a president who self-evidently is an alien, no longer even in disguise!"

Pandemonium ensues. We go back to BWN anchors while the moderator battles to win back control.

"Well, that is one way to break out of the crowd. We will take you back to the debate once the moderator is back in control."

"Will the American people relate to that? The president's behaviour is already off the map. But so much for toning it down."

"Your guess is as good as mine. The moderator meantime seems to be back in control so back to the debate..."

Chapter 65

White House briefing room

Presidential spokesperson Stephanie Spicer strides out beside Jack, now looking fully alien.

Spicer says, "Mayor Flanders at the last Democrat debate suggested calling out the National Guard. The president agrees. The country is so divided, citizens exercising their Second Amendment rights are at risk. So at tonight's rally in Sacramento, he has instructed the National Guard to deploy. Dana Ansell, you have a question."

"Has the president done this with consent of the California Governor?"

"This president does not need the consent of the Governor. May I remind you of enforcement of civil rights going back to the 1950s, where the federal government took precedence over the state?"

"Are you equating this situation to civil rights? This is a crisis of the president's own making..."

"I did not offer a follow up. But I would point out that civil rights was, as you put it, a crisis of the then president's own making."

Pandemonium erupts and Spicer allows this to swirl for a while before turning and walking out.

Chapter 66

Coffee shop

Jane and Kurt are sitting at an isolated table in their now-regular coffee shop.

Kurt says, "I feel so powerless. We have good inside contacts in the FBI yet we are getting nowhere."

"Didn't Durham promise to do his best?"

"He did. But the problem is finding a criminal angle on the Supreme Court judges."

"So why are we seeing him now?"

"I would like one last try at keeping the FBI involved. If that fails, we will probably have to get the House interested. Find a way to get Jack's justices impeached."

"As well as Jack himself? Won't the Republicans block it in the Senate?"

"If the evidence is out, it will become a political price for the Republicans. And that is Durham's problem. As an FBI agent, he can't get into anything partisan."

Durham walks in and sits down just as the waiter brings two cappuccinos. He orders. "Short black thanks," and waits for the waiter to leave.

"OK, I've been thinking. Kernighan died very publicly, talking as if he's an alien. That gives us cause to check out his DNA. That's as far as we can go in the FBI: without probable cause we can't go after the other justices President Jack appointed."

Jane shakes her head. "So even if we know those judges are almost certainly aliens, there is nothing we can do?"

"The House can impeach judges. They have power to subpoena evidence. Including DNA tests."

Kurt says, "OK, that's a start. I don't have any connections in Congress though."

"What about your student's girlfriend?" asks Jane. "She seems well connected politically."

Kurt contemplates briefly. "Good idea. Even if her main contacts are in the protest movement, she may be able to reach a sympathetic member of the House."

Durham's coffee arrives. He adds sugar and stirs for longer than necessary. "That could work. Particularly if you can keep some air between you and the politicians, in case you are needed as an expert witness. I'm afraid I have to keep my hands clean and stay away from anything political."

Kurt says, "Once again, we dump it on the kids."

Durham knocks his coffee back. "I gotta go. This is as far as I can take it off the books. Good luck with the House."

Durham leaves and Kurt stares at his back as he heads for the door.

Jane breaks the silence. "I can't believe the FBI can't do more."

"I do have another contact. My vet buddy said she's not scared of getting fired and has been close to that a few times."

"Let's talk to the kids about the impeachment angle, but keep your FBI maverick option open."

Chapter 67

Breaking World News: BWN

The Democratic field has thinned by the final debate. There are two candidates on stage. BWN anchors set the scene before switching focus to the moderator.

"The final Democratic debate is about to start. At last, they have narrowed the field to two candidates."

"The pundits are calling it crazy versus calm. Senator Brickhill has extensive experience but is seen as a safe choice. Mayor Flanders only has small-town experience but is notably outspoken. Over to the moderator."

"We will take the opening statements in turn from my left. Senator Brickhill."

Brickhill looks grave, giving every appearance of having been coached on looking presidential. "Our country is in crisis. Whether the president is an alien reverting to type or a human who has somehow converted to alien form, his erratic behaviour threatens the security and future of our nation. Clearly, since we cannot rely on the Republican Senate to convict him, we are left with beating him in the election. That calls for a calm, measured approach and sound policy as we cannot risk losing the election on other issues."

The moderator says, "Mayor, your turn."

Flanders says, "I can't believe what I am hearing. This is more than a crisis, this is an existential threat to our country. We do not know the full extent of alien assets planted in government. We do not know what is going on in the conflict in the alien camp. This is not the time for a safe pair of hands; it is the time for someone who will fight for our survival. While the president and state governors wrangle over who controls the National Guard through the courts, we have no way to prevent a coup. Which is what this fake president clearly plans."

The debate audience goes bananas and it goes downhill from there, with the candidates shouting over each other, the moderator and the audience.

Chapter 68

Canadian alien camp

We start from an aerial view.

There are many crude shacks, further than the eye can see. Trash is randomly scattered. A small number of figures wanders aimlessly between shacks, as if seeking a purpose. The perimeter fence is the one thing that is soundly maintained.

Patrols are made up of heavily armed aliens, the one part of the camp showing purpose. A group forms up and bashes on the door of a shack. A human figure emerges and is bundled away.

Aliens in the shack burst out. There's a short firefight, blue fire lighting the drab scene.

It's over almost as soon as it started.

Chapter 69

Breaking World News: BWN

The anchor duo takes over focus from the event that is supposed to be a debate.

"We break briefly from the Democratic debate. A firefight has broken out in the Canadian alien camp across the border from Nebraska."

"It appears to be under control already. The dominant faction, whichever that is, still has the upper hand."

"Jake, what is odd is they appear to have apprehended a human."

"Correct. It isn't clear though, from the available footage, what happened to him after the firefight, apparently started by a group that was harbouring him."

We see a reprise of the scene in the Canadian alien camp and freeze on the human emerging from the shack, as his face turns towards the camera. Cy Campbell – evidently not known to the BWN anchors. "We have no news as to who that is. We will get back to that once we have more information. Meanwhile, back to the Democratic debate."

Focus switches back to the debate where chaos remains the one thing making steady progress.

Chapter 70

Speaker McNamara's office

Speaker McNamara ushers Kurt, Jamie and Karen into his office. They all take seats around a conference table. "Any coffee for anyone?" he asks, and get assents from Kurt and Karen. He gestures to an aide who goes to the coffee machine in the corner.

McNamara passes around the coffees then gets right to it. "OK, so you have this foolproof way of distinguishing human from alien, even aliens disguised as human. Is there anything I can subpoena that you can measure? Can you explain how you came by this method?"

Kurt says, "Cy Campbell, supposedly a lawyer sent by the Canadian embassy to represent the Canadian, Harper, is actually an alien disguised as a human, same as Jack. He took us to the mothership..."

McNamara interrupts. "That was you! Why did the FBI never make that public?"

Kurt shrugs. "Who knows. When Kernighan was shot, our rather less dramatic excursion was forgotten in the noise of getting us off the case."

"Getting you off the case?"

"I have good contacts in the FBI and we wasted a lot of time trying to work through them. Best guess: someone high up was blocking us."

McNamara asks, "More aliens?"

"I doubt it. Best information we have is that the only fake humans are Campbell, Jack and his Supreme Court nominees."

Karen adds, "He has enablers. His counsel Corleone has a long history, for example, of shady right-wing causes and his judge nominations were strongly supported by the religious right."

Jamie shakes his head. "What weird times. A trip to an alien ship drops off the news just like that."

McNamara grimaces. "Tell me about it. Every time we have an angle on Jack, something else pops up that chases it off the news. But what I need to know is what you can bring to the hearing."

"Speaking of weird times," Jamie adds, "remember that incident last night when the aliens appeared to abduct a human from the Canadian alien camp?"

McNamara nods. "Yes, I saw it but didn't pay attention. A problem for Canada."

Jamie says, "I am sure it was Cy Campbell."

"Interesting. But goings on between the aliens are a distraction right now. Back to what you can offer me. No distractions, please. Kurt, if you don't mind. My time is limited."

"We have DNA samples from the Canadian who was contaminated with alien DNA and can still use their weapons. We have a pure alien sample from the firefight when we escaped the mothership. We also have a sample from Jack, but we don't have a plausible story of how we obtained that."

"And a simple test to tell the variations apart," Jamie adds. "We can also take photos through a microscope and point out the differences. Just a matter of counting."

McNamara purses his lips. "I see. Look, write this up. We'll do our best to get it all into evidence. Our next session is tomorrow morning. How soon can you get this to me?"

Jamie says, "We have the science already written up. And Karen..."

"... can check it out for legalities and how best to put it." She finishes for him.

"Great, but my staff will also check it over so can you get it to me by midday?"

Kurt stands up, conveying urgency. "Meanwhile the National Guard is confined to barracks until lawsuits over their deployment play out. And Jack's judges are all most likely aliens..."

"Let me stop you right there. We are not going to impeach judges while we are dealing with the president. We have to take these things one at a time. That our president could be an alien is already totally unprecedented. His base

refuse to believe it no matter how obvious it is and going after his precious right wing judges would simply make it blow
up even faster."

Chapter 71

House impeachment hearing

Judiciary Committee Chair Jane Gingrich gavels the impeachment session to order. Present are various Representatives and Corleone. Kurt is in the witness chair.

Gingrich starts. "We have a new witness who has stepped forward. Professor Kurt Lowell will read his opening statement."

"Thank you. I am a professor of bioinformatics at Georgetown University. I have a PhD in computer science from Berkeley and another in biotech from Stanford. I served four tours in Afghanistan in a special forces unit that I may not name and was awarded two purple hearts. When I chose to serve my country and put myself at risk, I had no thought for my personal safety. My commander-in-chief represented my people. I am not so sure now."

The view zooms out to the BWN studio and the usual anchors.

"Jake, this is a witness of unimpeachable credibility."

"At an impeachment hearing? Apologies to viewers for what I am sure is unintended humour."

We zoom back in to the hearing.

Kurt is still speaking. "I was invited to study evidence that the president may be an alien by General Kingston, who knows me from my time in service. I was working on background to the Canadian's story – Harper – who was accused of assaulting the president. One Cy Campbell, claiming to be a lawyer appointed by the Canadian embassy, also turned out to be an alien."

Back to the BWN studio.

"I wonder where this is leading."

"Let's go back to the hearing."

Kurt is still going. "At a safe house, we were investigating the Canadian's DNA as well as that of Judge Kernighan. Campbell rescued us from an alien attack and took the Canadian and I, with my assistant, to the mothership, which he had moved to DC. He tried to recruit us to convert humanity to the alien cause. That cause did not include the president, who is part of a rebel faction. My colleague, the Canadian and I decided that it was not our choice to decide where humanity stood and we escaped. During this episode we were able to garner a sample of alien DNA. The samples we have enabled us to construct a simple test to differentiate alien DNA from purely human DNA."

Gingrich waits a moment then realizes that Kurt is done.

"Colonel, you have rather briefly summarized your statement rather than reading the whole thing out."

"I am used to summarizing key points. You all have the written statement. I will of course amplify anything that is unclear in response to questions."

Gingrich nods formally. "Good. Then each side will have 90 minutes and the ranking member and I may yield to their counsel."

An arbitrary Republican butts in: "I have a question..."

Gingrich says, "What is relevant is: you don't have the floor. Ranking member, your round of questions will follow mine."

"And I will yield to my colleague at that time."

Gingrich is firm. "No you will not. I will conduct this session according to the agreed rules. Ranking member, your time is yours or your counsel's."

We zoom out to the BWN studio and the anchor duo.

"Agreed of course by the majority."

"But that was the game in the Clinton impeachment. Nothing to see here. Move on."

We now zoom out another layer to the video embedded in Twitter and watch the usual tweet storm.

Jack fan @Jackfan: #DeepState conspiracy #WitchHunt!

The True Lib @deepStateBlue: And they caught a witch. Well done, Democrats.

Jack fan @Jackfan: PAFA! PAFA! The
greatest president ever. Putting
America First!

The True Lib @deepStateBlue: Putting
aliens first always! You mean.

Chapter 72

Jane's apartment

Jane gets the door. Kurt leads Jamie and Karen in. Master Jack is playing again.

Karen asks, "What's that playing?"

Kurt explains. "Old song. Somehow matches what's going on these days."

"Hard to know what's going on today. Or any other day." Karen puts a hand on Kurt's shoulder. "Kurt, great job with your testimony."

Jane shakes her head. "What was worse? Four tours in Afghanistan or facing down the Republicans?"

"Being shot and expecting to die makes dealing with that rabble a lot easier than you'd think."

Jane gives him a lingering hug. "To me you were really convincing."

"The Republicans will make up all kinds of issues about admissibility. If this was a court of law that would be a prob-

191

lem."

Jamie asks, "Is it, Karen?"

"Impeachment is not a court case. Public opinion will be a big factor. A bigger one is the Senate where the Republicans have a majority and none of them is capable of standing up to Jack. No matter what the Articles of Impeachment say or what the evidence is, they will acquit. No way the Democrats can swing enough of them to get to 67 votes."

"Your other FBI contact?" Jane asks Kurt.

"Won't even take my calls. Impeachment it is. All or nothing. So much for someone willing to get fired."

Beers are passed around. The mood lightens.

Jane says, "All we can do now is wait."

Chapter 73

Yet another PAFA rally

A Jack surrogate is yet again at the podium with the usual sea of bright orange PAFA hats; Jack is on very big screens, surrounding the stadium once more.

Jack Surrogate hollers: "Put America First Again! Yeah!"

Crowd chants: "PAFA! PAFA! PAFA!"

Jack Surrogate roars: "California can't shut down our Second Amendment rights! Show your weapons! Stop the communist Democrats!"

Crowd chants: "LOCK THEM UP! LOCK THEM UP!"

* * * *

Outside the PAFA rally: overflow PAFA-hats mill around, looking disappointed at not being in the main crowd, despite the ever-present image of Jack surrounding the outside space as well this time.

A TV interviewer asks one, "As a Jack supporter, why do you feel the need to defy open carry prohibition?"

"I don't want to live in a police state. Democrats are communists!"

"Some Jack supporters are talking about stopping the election. Do you agree?"

"Absolutely! Deep state is trying to steal the election! President Jack forever!"

*   *   *   *

We zoom out to the BWN studio.

We see two apparently incredulous anchors – what can't be topped in the Jack universe?

"Jake, let me get this straight. Jack supporters are opposed to a police state... and want to make Jack president for life."

"At what point do I need to explain that logic has ceased to be an American value? At least not in Jack's America."

Chapter 74

Senate impeachment trial

Chief Justice McCoot gavels the trial to order. "I call Senate Majority Leader Robertson to open proceedings."

Robertson stands. "I remind senators of the rules. No electronics, no talking, no leaving the room. The president's counsel has requested permission to make a brief opening remark. Counsel, you have the floor."

Corleone shuffles papers and gives every appearance of having something weighty to say. "The president wishes it to be made known that he regards this proceeding as totally illegitimate and I agree with him.

"As a matter of law, if a president believes his own re-election to be in the national interest, then he is entitled to act on that belief."

We zoom out to BWN studio and our two anchors look as if they have just discovered the meaning of "incredulous". Yet again. Today.

"Jake, did I just hear the president's Counsel arguing that he can do anything to ensure his re-election if he believes that to be in the national interest?"

"You most certainly did. We turn now to Stanford Law School constitutional law professor, Bradly Simms. Professor, is there any basis in law for what he just said?"

"Absolutely not. That is a small step from arguing that he should be president for life. If his re-election is in the national interest and that trumps any consideration of legality, why not simply call off the election? Our founders were very explicit that they did not want a monarchy."

The first anchor nods. "Back to the hearing. Counsellor Corleone is laying out his witness strategy."

We zoom in to the trial.

Corleone stares around the chamber aggressively, his bulk somehow conveying brute force rather than flab. "Since we do not regard this hearing as legitimate we want no witnesses and urge the Senate to respect that. We've heard enough farcical witnesses in the House and there is no reason to hear more. It is the responsibility of the House to make a case and they ducked that responsibility. They should not ask the Senate to do their job for them."

We are back in the BWN studio.

"Bradly, did the same counsellor forcefully argue against calling any witnesses in the House hearings?"

Simms frowns. "Absolutely. The president's legal team have done everything in their power to prevent testimony and documents from reaching the House."

The second anchor asks, "Why did the Democrats not

take every subpoena to court?"

"Good question," Simms says. "They did take some to court but it very quickly became evident that if they persisted with that, it would take years and the election is now less than a year off."

The anchors now alternate.

"So in practical terms the Democrats have punted the ball to the Republican Senate?"

"Yes. And it will be interesting to see if they drop it. The Democrats allege obstruction because of this behaviour but the Republicans don't want a protracted trial or to get on the wrong side of their own president."

"Won't this lose them swing voters?"

"It's a matter of what they fear more and right now it's Jack. Our sources close to the Republican camp say that the Democrats will not get enough votes to call witnesses and once you get to that point, it's game over."

"What about the testimony of Colonel Lowell? Or professor, as he prefers?"

"He's a compelling witness. A war hero, extremely smart and credible. He stood up exceptionally to aggressive questioning by the Republicans. However, with all other material witnesses blocked, his testimony is isolated and only really raises doubts about whether the president is human."

"And that couldn't be tested because he refused to supply a DNA sample."

Simms gets a word in finally. "I must say, as a law professor, it seems exceptionally odd to me to conduct a trial without witnesses but an impeachment trial is an odd kind of

trial, where a faction of the jury gets to run the case. This
is why I keep coming back to the point that this is all really
about politics, not law."

Chapter 75

Jamie and Karen's apartment

Jamie and Karen are watching the Senate trial.

Jamie turns off the TV. "We did our best. More than half of America believes Jack is an alien but his base believes everything he says."

"Even if it is a bunch of pings in a language they don't understand."

"On the mothership, Cy Campbell said something like factionalism is human stupidity. I am not sure we have yet plumbed the depths of that."

"All very well for him to say that, but the aliens seem to have run into similar problems."

"I wonder what happened to him and whether we made the right choice of not allying with him."

"Jamie, you really could not have made a choice for all of

humanity. I'm proud of all of you for doing the right thing. In any case, what could we have done to help his cause?"

"Maybe we understand human stupidity a bit better than he does."

"Understanding what it is does not stop it. What have we actually achieved? Even with Kurt's two PhDs and high contacts, we have essentially made no impact."

Chapter 76

Finally *it* happens

Once again, a Jack surrogate is at the podium, with the usual sea of bright orange PAFA hats and all manner of weapons being waved; Jack is the ubiquitous presence on many big screens, inside and out.

Jack Surrogate yells: "Put America First Again! Yeah!"

Crowd chants: "PAFA! PAFA! PAFA!"

Jack Surrogate elaborates: "Communist Democrats will never defeat our Jack!"

Crowd: "LOCK THEM UP! LOCK THEM UP!"

Jack Surrogate: "Show us your weapons!"

Crowd: "PAFA! PAFA! PAFA!" Rifles and handguns are waved like branches in the wind.

Jack Surrogate: "Good guys with guns! Defend democracy against the Democrats!"

Crowd: "PAFA! PAFA! GOOD GUYS WITH GUNS! GOOD GUYS WITH GUNS!"

Suddenly, out of nowhere, a gunshot rings out. There's pandemonium. Total chaos. Shots ring out in all directions. People are screaming, running, falling where they are shot and clutching at wounds.

A shot, aimed or not, takes out a Jack big screen. No one notices in the melee. Except of course all-seeing social media. It becomes one of the emblematic scenes of the night.

Tweets can only be imagined.

Really.

I am not doing this for you every time.

Chapter 77

Breaking World News: BWN

President Jack is at the podium in the White House briefing room. The press corps is there in numbers. Jack holds up a sheet of paper. Presidential spokesperson Stephanie Spicer strides out and stands beside Jack.

Spicer opens proceedings. "In view of the sad events tonight when lawless elements have interfered with citizens' right to open carry, this president has no option but to declare a state of emergency."

Jack waves his page, his characteristic signature very visible at the bottom. Pandemonium.

Spicer says, "Dana. You have a question."

"By what authority is the president declaring a state of emergency?"

"The National Emergencies Act defines what a president

can do. His main aim is to stabilize the situation while the National Guard cannot be deployed to ensure peace."

"But the president himself created the conditions..."

Spicer interrupts. "Please, Dana, that is so rude. I haven't offered you a follow up. Wendy. You have a question."

Garcia takes her turn. "If the National Guard is confined to barracks, what resources will the president deploy to ensure peace?"

Spicer says, "The aliens have agreed to assist where necessary. Strictly on an as-needed basis."

Absolute chaos erupts.

Spicer eventually gets control back. "The president is calling on his supporters to welcome them with open arms. To ensure safety of Second Amendment supporters, we are asking them to assemble at secure locations." Some minutes of chaotic attempts at asking a question end with: "Since I am not getting any more sensible questions this briefing is over."

She and Jack stride out.

Ansell says, "And they call *us* the enemy of the people."

We zoom out to the BWN studio and our regular pair of anchors.

"Jake, correct me if I am wrong, but did we just see the president's spokesperson announcing a coup supported by the aliens?"

"I am not sure how else to characterise it. We are getting reports countrywide of alien troop deployment with advanced weapons."

"And the presidents' 'good guys with guns' being herded

together like sheep?"

"Cheering them on. While being herded by aliens into 'patriot camps'."

We zoom out to multiple scenes of aliens in advanced-tech vehicles being cheered on by Jack fans, with protesters fleeing in terror. In other scenes, large numbers of armed civilians are being herded into enclosures, brandishing placards in the usual style:

PAFA

SECOND AMENDMENT FIRST

JACK FOREVER

NO TO COMMUNIST SHEEP

Back to the BWN studio.

One of our anchors has discovered new heights of incredulity. "How can so many of the American people be so stupid? This is..."

The TV picture fails dramatically.

You're a very strange man and I thank you, Master Jack

Chapter 78

Jane's apartment

Kurt, Jamie, Jane and Karen watch the TV dying.

Master Jack is playing in the background.

Karen looks grim. "That song is starting to freak me out."

"After what we just saw on TV, I don't think anything will freak me out again." Kurt shakes his head.

"Have you noticed," Karen goes on, "that Jackian talking heads refer to him as 'this president' as if he's one of a kind?"

Jamie says, "Isn't he? Aside from the alien thing, he does something unelectable every five minutes. During the election his apologists said it was an act and the 'presidential pivot' would happen any minute."

Jane snorts. "I am no expert on ballet but I can't visualize him as a ballerina."

Karen brings it back to practicalities. "That's a funny thought but what are we going to do?"

Jane looks at Kurt. "Stick with the dude who survived

four tours in Afghanistan. And came out relatively sane."

"I can't think of a better plan," Jamie adds.

Kurt breaks a long silence. "I damn well wish someone would. Because I have fuck all idea what to do next."

The lights fail. There are blue flashes and screams outside.

Chapter 79

DC camp

We start from an aerial view.

There are many crude shacks, further than the eye can see. Trash is randomly scattered. A small number of figures wanders aimlessly between shacks, as if seeking a purpose. The perimeter fence is the one thing that is soundly maintained.

We zoom out. The Washington Monument and Capitol are in the distance.

Now we zoom down to a shack. A convoy of aliens approaches in Hummers. Ten aliens emerge from vehicles, heavily armed. On closer inspection, one is not armed and is human: Thomas Harper.

The lead alien pounds on the door, almost knocking it off its makeshift hinges. Jamie's face emerges.

"PING PING PING PING PING PING PING!"

Harper breaks into a sunny grin. "Hey, I didn't know it

was you. Report of aliens hidden here. You have nothing, right?"

Jamie says sharply, "Uh, no. Of course not. Just here with my girlfriend. How did you..."

"This bunch never got out of the Canadian camp, only dealt with the cheap Hispanic help we brought in from the US. So they don't understand English so good. Need an interpreter." Harper gestures at his alien bosses.

"Always land on your feet."

"What can I do? It's this or..." He gestures vaguely around the camp.

The lead alien shows signs of impatience: "PING PING PING PING PING PING PING PING!"

Harper says, "*No lo conozco.* Telling them I don't know you. I think. My Spanish isn't so hot either."

Lead Alien says, "PING PING PING PING PING PING PING PING PING PING."

"*Solo mi cara en la tele,*" Harper says to the alien. "This guy saw my face on the TV."

Jamie says, "Yeah, right, your face on the TV. Saw you a few times."

Harper turns back to the lead alien. "*Nada – dirección incorrecta.*" Then to Jamie: "Telling them wrong address."

The lead alien responds with, "PING PING PING PING PING!" and gestures impatiently.

"OK, I have to move on." Harper and the aliens pile into Humvees and leave in a cloud of dust.

Karen emerges when it is clear that the unwanted visitors are nowhere near. "Sweet. We have an address now. Could you let us know the street name and number?"

"Sadly, they left before I could ask."

Kurt emerges. "That was too close. We must move. We've had so much luck so far – escaping the chaos of the collapse of government, no aliens picking up that we could be a threat before we had time to take refuge here."

Two aliens emerge, followed by Jane.

Jane says, "I wonder how the Canadian would feel if he knew Juan and Antonio were safe and well."

"Not so safe here any more." Jamie shakes his head.

"Yup," adds Kurt. "They're conspicuous here for the same reason we found them. Aliens are scarce here in this useless humans dump."

"Who would have guessed that the alien faction basing its tactics on human stupidity would win?" Karen asks.

Antonio says, "PING PING PING PING PING PING PING!"

Juan, not to be left out, adds, "PING PING."

"You remind me of that thing of Cy's," Jamie acknowledges. "What was it? Unity. Power. One species, one goal."

Kurt grins wryly. "A bit like our *E pluribus unum*. I'm not sure if that applies any more either. I wonder what Latin is for *stupidity rules*."

One more figure emerges from the shack. Cy Campbell.

"Yes, who would have guessed... Human stupidity, the most powerful force in the universe."

You're a very strange man and I thank you... Master Jack

Acknowledgements

I would like to thank David Marks, who wrote Master Jack, for encouraging me to use the lyrics.

My incomparable wife Fiona Semple pointed out obvious errors as did others who prefer to be anonymous.

Gunda Spingies provided an efficient and professional proofreading service.

I claim ownership of any residual errors.